THE BIG CASINO

THE BIG CASINO

Merrill K. Albert

VANTAGE PRESS
New York

This is a work of fiction. Any similarity between the characters appearing herein and any real persons, living or dead, is purely coincidental.

FIRST EDITION

Copyright © 2000 by Merrill K. Albert

Published by Vantage Press, Inc.
516 West 34th Street, New York, New York 10001

Manufactured in the United States of America
ISBN: 0-533-13267-3

Library of Congress Catalog Card No.: 99-95017

0 9 8 7 6 5 4 3 2 1

To the residents of the City of Carmel, California:

Thank you for the privilege of using your hospitable public library wherein I found the inspiration for writing much of this book. Virginia Woolf would quite understand when I say that in this library I found "a room of my own."

Contents

Preface

After this book was accepted by Vantage Press for publication and before the completion of its printing, an astounding archaeological find was announced which, together with other subsequent events and happenings, made necessary the preparation of this Preface. This find and other events will be discussed in their order of importance but, before doing so, allow me to present a brief overview of the Egypt chapter and the theories therein. This chapter sets forth three theories about Egypt:

1. That the culture and history of Egypt has been profoundly impacted by the culture and philosophy of ancient China;

2. That in prehistoric times (defined as that period of time between the end of the last Ice Age and the invention of writing) there existed an extensive and protracted cultural and technological interchange between Egypt and the Asiatic peoples of Meso-America; and

3. That the pyramids of Egypt and the Sphinx were designed and constructed by technology and stone masonry skills borrowed from the Asiatic peoples of Meso-America and imported into Egypt. This theory includes the concept that skilled workers (architects, master stone masons and skilled laborers) were imported into Egypt from Meso-America.

Now, let us turn to the archaeological find and to the subsequent events which I consider bear directly upon these theories. They are as follows:

a. In August 1999 I watched a television program prepared by the British Broadcasting Corporation-London and presented to the American audience. This program concerned a British scientific expedition to Bolivia to examine and explore a series of ancient canals built in the form of concentric circles which seemed to be connected to an ancient river system which eventually emptied into the Atlantic Ocean. A British scientist, who had retired from the Royal Air Force as a reconnaissance expert, had expressed the idea that this area might be the site of Atlantis. This expedition failed to find any evidence to support the reasons presented for undertaking it but the program's narrator made this statement: "Several scientists recently have made claim to finding cocoa leaves within the burial garments of Egyptian mummies from pharoanic times." Since the cocoa plant is found only in the Andes, it struck me that this appeared to be considerable proof of some sort that an ancient cultural connection had indeed occurred between these civilizations which are separated by the expanse of the Atlantic Ocean. Moreover, this program included a personal appearance by and interview of Thor Heyerdahl. The interviewer asked Mr. Heyerdahl about the Ra voyages of 1970 which Heyerdahl made from near the Canary Islands to the Caribbean in a primitive boat made of reeds. Here is what Thor Heyerdahl said: "I made the Ra voyages not to prove that the Egyptians made such a voyage to Meso-America, but to prove that such a voyage was possible."

After seeing this program I attempted to and did contact Thor Heyerdahl (he lives in the Canary Islands). I sent him a letter setting forth the theories I have outlined in this Preface and asked for his comments on the cocoa plant find. On the issue as to whether the ancient Egyptians had made voyages of discovery to the Americas, he said: "Personally, I believe that the Egyptians confined themselves to navigation on the Nile from the time the pharoahs settled along these river banks some 5,000 years ago. After that time, they collaborated with Phoenicians in ocean voyages. There is very strong evidence to believe that people from North Africa or the Mediterranean area crossed the tropical belt prior to the Europeans, but the relationship cannot at the present be pinned down to a definite period or cultural group." On the issue of the cocoa leaves finding, Mr. Heyerdahl said, "Recently several scientists have claimed to have found evidence of American drug plants in mummies from pharoanic times. This problem is still under discussion, and one has to be careful until conclusive information is available."

I will honor Thor Heyerdahl's caveat and make no claim that the cocoa leaf finding proves any theory I have proposed. I urge only that this find should encourage further study and archaeological exploration upon the controversial point whether the civilizations of Egypt and Meso-America did interact in antiquity.

b. The prevailing winds and currents in that portion of the Atlantic between the Straits of Gibraltar and the Caribbean Islands make a westward voyage of exploration by an early sailing vessel a relatively safe passage. This is forcefully expressed in Heyerdahl's book, *Early Man and the Ocean.* Heyerdahl uses the wonderfully descriptive word "conveyor" to describe the effect of winds and the Gulf Stream current upon westward transatlantic voyages. Simply stated, he makes the case that any type of a seaworthy sailing vessel could or would be "conveyed" by such winds and currents from the Straits of Gibraltar to the Caribbean and return.

Now let us consider any possible historical proof of this theory. Five hundred years ago, Columbus made three voyages from Europe to Meso-America and returned without mishap, aided only by the crude navigational instruments of that time. Similar voyages were made by Cortez, Pizarro, and Ponce de Leon.

Concerning the comparative ease of such voyages, consider the accomplishment of a Kentucky woman, Tori Murden, who, in December 1999, completed a solo voyage from the Canary Islands to Guadeloupe in the Caribbean Islands. She rowed her 27-foot rowboat 3000 miles across the Atlantic. To all of this, add a new theory—the Solutrean Theory—proposed in September 1999 by Dr. Dennis Stanford to an archaeological conference held in New Mexico. This theory argues that people from Spain and France (Caucasians) may have reached the Americas from Europe as long ago as 16,000 years. This is the theory alluded to in Mr. Thor Heyerdahl's letter to me.

c. Many years ago, America's most famous mystic made several prophecies (or readings, if you will) concerning the Sphinx and the pyramids of Egypt. In one of his readings, Edgar Cayce said that the pyramids were built in 10,500 B.C. In another reading, Cayce prophesied that "secret chambers" would be found in the paws of the Sphinx and that underground passageways would be found beneath the pyramids and the Sphinx. He also prophesied that in these secret chambers or passageways would be found "a hall of records." These readings of Edgar Cayce have been receiving renewed interest and currency by the archaeological community because of the fact that recent X rays of both the pyramids of Giseh and the Sphinx have revealed that such secret chambers and passageways do exist.

I asked Charles Thomas Cayce, President of the Edgar Cayce Foundation of Virginia Beach, Virginia, to look at the chapter of my book entitled "Egypt and the Legend of Atlantis" with the idea in mind whether the theories and ideas I presented were in general harmony with those of Edgar Cayce on the basic premise that there was a definite and prolonged connection between these ancient cultures. Mr. Cayce agreed and proofs of this chapter were sent directly by the publisher to Mr. Cayce's foundation. Here is what Mr. Cayce said: "I have finally had an opportunity to look at the chapter, 'Egypt and the Legend of Atlantis' from your book manuscript, *The Big Casino.* I think you do a good job of raising questions about the traditional views of early civilizations and possible alternative explanations of the developments of some of those ancient cultures. As you probably know, your ideas are not exactly along the lines of the Cayce readings, but the basic premise that there were connections between these ancient civilizations, and that these civilizations are perhaps much older and more advanced than much past information seems to indicate, certainly fits the general concepts of the readings on these subjects."

d. The Egyptian Government has just recently completed a general cleaning up and overhaul of the Sphinx. As earlier indicated, x-ray examination was made of the Sphinx and the pyramids. Egyptologists have confirmed that secret chambers, etc. exist and examination of these chambers and passageways are underway. It has been said that the archaeological community can expect a major announcement as to what has been discovered "by the end of the year 2000."

There is an old Arabic proverb which goes like this: "Man fears time and time fears the pyramids."

I ask the reader to allow the mind to pause in reflection upon the mystery which attends these magnificent structures. There are 95 pyramids in Egypt. There are more than 100,000 pyramids in Mexico alone, most of which have never been examined by an archaeologist.

Why is it that one cannot find in Egypt any earlier, more elementary predecessor pyramids which would give us insight to their evolution? As many historians and Egyptologists have said, the pyramids appear to have been built in a vacuum. Others have described both the pyramids and the Egyptian civilization itself to have appeared to have arisen in the desert like a phoenix. And what will the scholars say when the rumored finding of a pyramid in Meso-America, older than that of the first pyramid of Egypt (Sakkara), is confirmed?

We can but wait, with both anticipation and wonderment, to learn what secrets have been uncovered by the industry of the spade. Perhaps a new chapter in the ever amazing history of Egypt is about to be written.

I wish to express my thanks and gratitude to both Thor Heyerdahl and Charles Thomas Cayce for their comments and advice.

—The Author

I

The Big Casino

The most important day in the life of Maxwelton Allenby had begun. Walking to his car, he noticed that a bright May morning sun had coated the streets of Lido Isle with a patina of gold. It seemed as if Providence had decreed that everyone on earth "have a great day," everyone, that is, save Allenby. On this day Allenby (Max, as he was known) was to learn whether his cancer, recently discovered, was curable or not.

The streets of the island had cleared of morning traffic, and the offshore breezes of the Pacific had carried away all remnants of smog. It was clear and calm and Allenby was in no hurry; indeed, he was a bit reluctant to get to his hospital appointment. Arriving at his garage, he stopped to take stock of his life.

Max considered himself blessed by good fortune. He was in the culminating time of his life. He had just entered his forties, his law practice was flourishing, and his home, though modest by the standards of Newport Beach, was located on one of most desired islands of the community. He had failed at marriage, yet he had gained a bright and loyal daughter, whom he had named Amy. In short, it seemed that Allenby had everything.

This had all changed about six months ago when he began to feel ill and weak. Then he began to tire earlier and earlier each day and noticed that at each morning it seemed more difficult to get out of bed and get going. His color took on a pale and somewhat unhealthy look, like that of a person coming down with the flu. He thought perhaps he had been working too hard.

Then it happened. The first ominous signal of this silent disease became manifest one morning. His urine contained obvious streaks of blood. Alarmed, and aware of this evil portent, he made an immediate appointment with Dr. Thomas Wallenscroft, the head of the Department of Oncology at Hoacks Hospital. Dr. Wallenscroft ordered all appropriate tests including stool samples, which likewise contained the feared marker—blood. X rays of the body were taken, MRI scans run and blood samples sent out for evaluation. A full clinical work-up having been completed, Dr. Wallenscroft arranged to have Allenby's file evaluated by two outstanding oncologists at Good Samaritan Hospital in Los Angeles. Today was the day on which the final prognosis was to be made. Allenby had made a personal vow that he would not retreat into self-pity if it was unfavorable. With a sigh and heavy of heart, he got into his car and headed toward the appointment.

Hoacks Hospital sat on a large bluff facing west toward the Pacific Ocean. It had been constructed in that atrocious hospital architectural style so befuddling to its patients, that color coding painted on the hallway floors was needed to enable negotiation of its dreary maze. The hospital had originally been intended for the care and treatment of industrial injuries, but its owners early on saw that real money could be made in administering to the dying. Further, medical statistics revealed with increasing clarity that the great majority of cancer patients were "older"—loosely defined as those patients over sixty. This meant, of course, that Medicare presented a painless solution to the problem of payment of bills.

Over the years the hospital had evolved into a facility that treated a vast number of cancer patients, and the upper three floors of the structure became known as "the cancer wards." In fact, many of the hospital's critics claimed that this was done so that the onshore breezes of the ocean could waft the moans of the patients getting chemotherapy treatment onto those areas of the community occupied by the less affluent. Allenby parked his car in the patients' lot and headed to Dr. Wallenscroft's office on the eighth floor. It took a considerable personal resolve to put on a tolerably pleasant face as he entered the office.

Dr. Wallenscroft's office was large by medical standards, and four solemn patients sat waiting. He could see the outline of a receptionist behind a glass partition, and he took a seat and waited. Allenby took particular pains to appear not to be staring at the other patients, but he sneaked a look or two at each of them when possible and noticed that each of the patients had one obvious thing in common. The eyes of each and every patient had a haunted and stricken look, screaming of the terror and foreboding that lay within.

Eventually, a door opened and Dr. Wallenscroft's receptionist entered the waiting room. Allenby was thunderstruck! The receptionist was a raving beauty, blonde, young, with a ravishing figure, which shouted its abundant good health. Allenby began to wonder if this was another of Wallenscroft's attempts at a joke. The receptionist came directly to where Allenby sat and said, "Are you Mr. Allenby?" Allenby acknowledged that he was and was ushered immediately into the doctor's office.

Dr. Wallenscroft was alone in his office and rose immediately to greet his friend and patient. They had become tennis friends and partners at the Newport Beach Tennis Club, which featured a very active aprés tennis life, catering to numerous young women looking for an attractive professional male. Both Allenby and Wallenscroft were very active at the busy bar of this club and were much in demand at the cocktail hour.

Dr. Wallenscroft took a seat and motioned to Allenby to sit down. A few perfunctory remarks passed between the two men. "How is your game?" "Did you watch that match between X and Y?" This made Allenby even more apprehensive because he knew, intuitively, that Wallenscroft was most reluctant to get to the point.

At length, the doctor opened a thick medical file bearing his name and said, "Allenby, we have given you every test known to oncological science and every x-ray evaluation known to us, and we are unanimous in our opinion. Before giving you my final prognosis, I would like to give you some good news and some bad news. Which do you want first?"

Allenby said, "Doc, give me the good news first."

Wallenscroft replied, "Okay, did you see that gorgeous blonde in my reception room?"

Allenby said, "I certainly did."

Wallenscroft said, "The good news is, I'm fucking her."

Stunned, Allenby said, "And the bad news?"

Wallenscroft replied, "The bad news is that you have drawn the Big Casino; it is all over your pancreas and liver, and it appears to have invaded your lower rib cage. It appears to all of us to be terminal."

An ominous silence came upon the doctor's office, and each man sat staring into space. At first Allenby was outraged by Wallenscroft's insensitive joke and even further put off by what was, to him, a ghastly prognosis presented in an almost casual manner. He reasoned that perhaps the doctor's unfortunate manner had been crafted by viewing episodes of "MASH" or after having read *One Flew Over the*

Cuckoo's Nest. He decided that anger would accomplish nothing, so gathering every bit of composure remaining within him, he said, "How long have I got and what can be done?"

Wallenscroft as last realized that his manner had wounded his patient and, putting on his most professional and articulate mask, he said, "The only treatment we have at this stage of your illness is chemotherapy, coupled with radium treatments. If this course of treatment puts the disease into remission, you may live as long as five years. If you do nothing, I doubt that you can last one year."

Allenby, remembering his self-imposed promise to bear whatever news that came with dignity, stood up and said, "Thank you for your treatment and advice, and allow me time to think it over." Without another word, he left the office and drove home to Lido Isle.

II

The Decision

Upon entering his home, Max put on a pot of coffee, took off his suit and shoes, and got comfortable in his robe and slippers. Soon refreshed, he recognized the need to make an accounting of his new situation and to come to terms with this ominous change in his future. He called his office, told his secretary that he was "ill," and would be out for the remainder of the week. That done, he went into his den, stretched out on his couch to put into use the brain that had helped him sort out so many difficult problems in the past.

In his youth Max had gone to sea for several years (obtaining a Mate's license) before completing university and law school. The experience at sea, coupled with that learned as a trial attorney, had taught him that he must assemble all of the facts bearing upon any problem he faced. The course thus charted, he took the next several days to ponder the matter and to find a solution.

Max did not have to start from scratch. He had known for more than six months that he had some sort of cancer but never for an instant felt that he was dying. He accepted that he had looked a bit pale and seemed to tire easily, but he had not lost significant weight and still retained his athletic and muscular build. There were days when he felt almost normal, but those days were inevitably followed by days during which he knew something was definitely wrong. He constantly wondered why he had never experienced any pain, why a disease that ostensibly was killing him progressed through his body with scarcely a trace.

Max called upon his experiences with friends who had died from cancer. Five such friends had died, each had undergone extensive periods of chemotherapy and radiation, and none had obtained any benefits whatsoever. What is more, Max had noted that the last months in the life of each were filled with pain and discomfort and were totally devoid of even the most basic human pleasures.

Max had feverishly researched whether there was a reasonable chance that a cure could be found before he died. He had spoken to every doctor of his acquaintance on this subject, read every paper available at the county medical library, and had found that medical science had not even decided the cause of cancer! He marveled that the public had been inundated by such statements as "Smoking causes cancer," without any explanation whatsoever why millions of smokers across the world never contract the disease. He constantly pondered the riddle as to why children would suffer and die from cancer each day, though each had never smoked or drank or put any harmful substance into their bodies.

It was from such thought and research that Allenby concluded that chemotherapy was not the answer, save in an exceptional case, and that medical science might be on the wrong track. It was his conclusion that cancer was within every living person and that it was set off either by a form of cellular or genetic "mutiny" or by a failure of the body's natural immune system, or perhaps by defects in diet.

Days upon days followed as Max wrestled with his problem. Days of hope were followed by days during which Max reached the conclusion that his personal gift of life was about to be returned to its maker. He ultimately decided that he did not want to end life living days that held neither happiness nor hope, but only pain and despair. He had made up his mind. He wanted to end his life on his terms rather than submit to the cruel protocol of the disease.

III

The Final Voyage

In the days following his decision, Max experienced a feeling that approached elation. Perhaps "elation" is not quite the word. Perhaps "relief" is better suited to explain the state of mind of one who had faced, and made, the ultimate decision of his life.

Max called his office and explained the situation to his staff. He did not want to burden them with his personal problems, so he chose to explain that his doctor had recommended a "sabbatical" be taken to restore his health. Each of his cases was returned to the client, appropriate bonuses paid to the staff, and his law practice was closed. Allenby had already taken care of his will and made arrangements for the disposition of his home. The only problem remaining was how to make the graceful exit.

Allenby had confided his condition to but one person, his daughter. The time had come to implement that decision; he had made up his mind to die at sea. He had nothing but pleasant memories of his seafaring days and never felt closer to a full life experience than when facing the implacable forces that control the actions of the sea. He had always found the stars in their correct place in the universe whenever he used his sextant. He had always noticed that every storm, however brutal, eventually ended and that the barometer faithfully foretold the changes in weather that impended. In a word, there was some eternal order at work and if he were to die, he wanted some semblance of life's order to preside over the event.

Max decided to book passage on one of those passenger liners calling at Los Angeles. It was his plan to jump overboard during the middle of the night at a time and place of his choosing. Before doing so, however, he wanted company, knowing as he did, that these voyages were very festive, so he telephoned Amy at San Francisco, told her of his plans, and asked her to come along. Amy knew that her father thought he was dying, so she readily agreed and made appropriate arrangements to rendezvous with him on board. Max found that the liner *Amsterdam* of the Holland American Lines was leaving Los Angeles in a month and booked a stateroom for two. The *Amsterdam* was to depart Los Angeles, pass through the Panama Canal, cruise up the Eastern Seaboard, and then turn east to Southampton, England. The ship was the flag ship of a fleet run by one of the world's premier steamship companies. It was renowned for its service, the quality of its crew, and the cleanliness of each ship. Allenby decided that if he were to "go," it would be in First Class.

The day of departure had finally arrived, and Max and Amy met at the gangplank an hour prior to departure. Max had never seen his daughter look better and told her so. Amy carefully examined her father, expecting to see obvious signs of an on-rushing death. She feared that his skull might be pushing through the skin that covered it. She dreaded facing the possibility that his body might have begun to shrivel. She was astonished! Though pale and appearing to be a bit tired and dispirited, he looked vigorous and athletic. "Dad," she exclaimed, "you look great!"

Allenby managed a weak smile and said, "Let's go to our cabin." Allenby had decided not to tell Amy that he was going to commit suicide during the voyage. He told her that he would give her the details of their adventure when they were settled in.

The *Amsterdam* was a liner of medium size, which carried approximately five hundred passengers. The ship had been made more comfortable by having only two passenger decks—one First Class and the other Second Class. Large passageways and comfortable stairways had made moving about the ship a joy, and soon they were in Stateroom 10—First Class. Max opened the door to Stateroom 10 and told Amy to enter. The scene that met her eyes was one of incomparable luxury. A large and tastefully outfitted sitting room was first entered, complete with bar, a writing desk, and a beautiful cocktail table. The room in turn led to two separate bedrooms, each with its own bath and toilet facilities. It was as if one could go on an ocean cruise while in a suite at the Waldorf-Astoria.

By this time the sounds of a cruise ship preparing to leave port were heard. Shouts of sheer excitement and joy in the prospects of the commencing adventure could be heard from hundreds of the passengers lining the rails, and the final departure warnings were announced to those not taking the voyage. Presently, Max felt the unmistakable movement of the great ship getting underway as the tugs moved it away from its berth into the channel leading to open sea. Allenby's final voyage had begun.

The first thing Max did was to call for tea, for he wanted to give Amy an overview of the voyage and his reasons for requesting her company. The tea tray promptly came. Max and Amy stowed their luggage away and sat down to their first father-daughter talk since Max had learned that his cancer could not be cured.

Amy began the conversation. "You know, Dad, you didn't have to spend all this money on me. This must have cost a bundle."

Max replied, "Do you know of a better time for me to spend my money?" No rejoinder being possible, Amy waited to hear out her father. A long silence ensued as each fussed with the tea service. Finally, Max began, "I have arranged our cruise because I wanted to give you a complete picture of my medical problem and ask only that you listen until I have set it out. Amy, I am dying of cancer. It is in both my pancreas and liver and growths have been detected on my ribs. I have consulted with the leading oncologists of the community, and each has said that the disease has spread so extensively any hope for either a remission or a cure is not reasonable. The only treatment offered is to undergo continuous chemotherapy and radiation in order to give me a few more years of life. The prospect of living that kind of existence is not acceptable, and I decided to go to England to try one last treatment—herbal medicine at the University of London." Unable to tell his daughter of his decision to commit suicide during the voyage, he concluded by saying, "In the meantime, we will have a few glorious weeks together and let's make the most of it."

During all the time her father had spoken, Amy had cried softly and her face had shaped into a sorrowful mask. Nonetheless, she was determined to explore the other side of the situation and replied, "How do you know that there is no cure or that one might not be found any day? You have always told me, since the beginning, that you believe that cancer is within us since birth and that some unknown biological agent sets it off. If that is the case, could not some instant remission or cure occur for whatever reason? What about the miracles at Lourdes, Dad? The waters have been tested by every method known to modern science, found to be ordinary mountain spring water, yet miracles still occur.

And how do you know that your doctors may not be wrong in this case? You certainly don't look like you are dying."

A shy smile lit her father's face. "I'm certainly glad I brought you along. Let's let it rest for a while and get on with the cruise."

The days that followed were filled with every conceivable pleasure. The ship's company had arranged for something amusing or adventurous to occur all day long. Allenby occupied himself with afternoons at bridge, an occasional swim, sessions in the gym, and early evening walks on the promenade deck with Amy. For the evening meal, the ship had provided an interesting diversion. Seating for the evening's dining was done by random choice by the ship's steward so that conversation at each meal was a new experience. The *Amsterdam's* passenger list was loaded with single women on holiday, and dancing and conversation were available for the asking. Games of chance at modest stakes were made available in the lounge, which throbbed with excited conversation and music until midnight. Allenby seemed to win at every game of chance, to hold the strongest cards at bridge, to find the most exciting woman to converse with. He began to wonder—is this voyage a sort of epiphany?

Days of pleasure followed swiftly one upon the other until Allenby began to feel that his sense of time was becoming blurred. He noticed that his color had returned to normal and that his appetite for life seemed almost insatiable. At length, the *Amsterdam* began its approach toward Key West and his rendezvous with death.

The ship's captain had announced that day that dinner was to be a black-tie affair to celebrate both the meeting of the ship with the Gulf Stream and its imminent arrival at the Port of Miami for a three-day layover. This was the night that Allenby had waited for. He had decided to jump overboard at midnight. He made arrangements for a table for two so that he could, at last, tell Amy of his final decision.

Dinner started at eight, and the main dining room resounded with conversation and music. Flowers and party decorations were everywhere, and it became immediately apparent that the occasion, entitled, "Dining on the Gulf Stream," was a smash. The steward's department had exceeded even the extravagant reputation of the shipping company, and presentation of the various courses took several hours. Dancing music played on through the evening, and Allenby made certain to use his last chance to dance with Amy. Several of his women friends came to the table to ask Allenby to dance, but he put them off on the pretext that he did not feel well. Glancing at his watch, he saw that midnight was approaching so he told Amy he had something important to say.

The dining table had been cleared and father and daughter sipped an after-dinner drink each looking at the other. Allenby had never seen his daughter looking lovelier. Her skin shone and her young body fought against the restraints of her evening dress. Her eyes glistened with the expectations created by the evening, and every fiber of her being exuded that good health that had fled his body. He decided to get to the point.

"Amy," he said, "I'm going to commit suicide tonight and I beg you to say not a word. I have thought over this situation for many months and want to end life on my terms rather than upon those set by a cruel and unbeatable disease. Please come with me." Amy was thunderstruck. All the joy of the evening fled her face, but she knew that her father meant every word he had just spoken. The two arose from the table, and Allenby led the way back to the stateroom.

Allenby went into the stateroom, strapped a package he had previously prepared to his chest, and put back on his tuxedo jacket. Taking Amy by the hand, he slowly walked toward the stern until he reached the stern railing. Not a soul was about and the only sounds that could be heard were the pounding of the engines and the great churning sounds of the two propellers. In the background faint noises from the dining room indicated that the evening's festivities continued.

Allenby turned to Amy and said, "I love you with all my heart and soul. Everything I own has been left to you and there are written instructions for you in my room. Don't tell anyone about this until tomorrow morning. Now, please go back to the stateroom." Allenby kissed her good-bye on both cheeks and Amy turned and was gone. Allenby stood alone at the taffrail. In a moment the ship's bridge sounded eight bells. Midnight had come. He climbed to the top rail, took a mighty jump, and plunged into the churning wake of the *Amsterdam*.

Allenby landed feet first into the foaming propeller wash left by the *Amsterdam*. He plunged straight down and saw that the color of the Gulf Stream began to change from bubbly white to deeper and deeper shades of black. His body seemed to provide no resistance to his fall. The laws of buoyancy seemed suspended, and he felt as if he had stepped into a bottomless elevator shaft. For a mad moment he thought, *How could man have possibly originated in the oceans? I have no defense whatsoever against the forces that are about to kill me.*

Soon his body began its reaction to the forces of the universe that provide a canopy of pressure over the sea. His heart began to race and pound against the confines of his rib cage; his lungs began to ache and his eyes pressed against their sockets. He remembered the lessons learned in a pamphlet prepared by a certain Doctor Q. It was called, "Feed the Sharks: Let's Not Fill Up the Cemeteries." The paper recommended death by drowning at sea upon the principal ground that it avoided the messy problem of dealing with the corpse. Ten steps were set out, the chief of which was, at the final moment, to open one's mouth and nostrils to the limit and suck in the ocean water so as to fill the lungs instantaneously. That moment had come.

In a microsecond remaining within the few moments he had to live, an astonishment occurred. Try as he might, he could not force open his mouth! Using every contortion he knew, activating every facial muscle he controlled, he could not get his nostrils to open! Simply put, the command of his mind to die had been countermanded by a command from his autonomous system to live. Those ancient signals to cling to life, pressed upon his personal genetic code in the age of stone, now kicked in. In his mind, Allenby thought he had undergone a form of chrysalis. He had emerged from the pupal stage of the quitter into that of a survivor. In a flash his descent into darkness ended.

His legs, without any command from Allenby, now began a violent frog kick. His arms began a climbing motion as if he were ascending a ladder of liquid. Up and up he spiraled as each second brought unbearable pain to his lungs. He feared he would never make it but, at last, the water above began to lighten, and with a violent pop, his head broke the plane of the ocean's surface. With great gulps, his lungs sucked in the elixir of life.

Allenby was a mess. His arms ached, his legs felt encased in concrete, and his head and lungs still throbbed from the ordeal. He called upon the simple life-saving instructions learned as a Boy Scout in his youth and began a slow dog paddle. Looking about, he saw that the *Amsterdam* had already merged with the darkness of the night. Round and round he slowly circled, and the stupidity of his decision to die began to meld into the hopelessness of his situation.

All night long Allenby made a slow circle in the waters of the Gulf Stream. Each hour of the night seemed to glide into the other with no change. No ships came by, no fish circled about. Like a distant star, he was in his own universe. As the night dragged endlessly on, he again confronted feelings that he would not survive. Weariness began to cover him like a shroud.

At last, the forces of nature began its process of illuminating the world. He looked toward what he believed to be the east and saw that the horizon had begun to lighten. Within moments the upper rim of the sun peeked above the horizon and sent its rays racing upon the flat plane of the Caribbean. As if by magic, the sea came alive and he cast his eyes about to survey the scene.

Suddenly, he saw it. Straight ahead and not one hundred yards away, a large object bobbed about in the water. Summing all of his will and whatever strength remained, he paddled toward it. Arriving alongside, he saw that it was a rectangular wooden crate used on merchant ships to contain fruit. Calling upon every reserve left in his exhausted body he heaved himself upon it, collapsed face down, and passed out.

IV

Anne's Quest

A warm May day had commenced upon the crowded streets of Manhattan as Anne Arpels, model extraordinaire, walked toward the Middlethrope Agency on Park Avenue. She was its superstar and the embodiment of that new trend in female modeling—a wholesome, athletic American girl with a smashing body. The anorexic type was not her game; gigs that required the model to be a walking coat hanger were left to others. She had risen to the very top of her profession by daring to be, and to portray, a woman not only beautiful but capable of taking on any adventure that life might afford.

Anne had chosen to dress conservatively because she was to meet with agency head Lisa Middlethorpe to announce a decision. A gorgeous blue sailor suit with hat did its best to conceal the treasure of Arpel's body. Nothing created by the fashion industry of man could conceal what creation had designed to be observed. If concealment was the purpose of the outfit, it failed miserably, and male after male stared, whistled, and applauded as she strode purposefully toward the agency. It was just such attention she had grown to dislike, and she hurried along to get off the street and into the sanctuary of the agency.

Arpels was ushered into Middlethorpe's suite, and the two women who had not seen each other in more than six months faced off. Lisa (Middy, as she was known in the world of fashion) moved forward, embraced Arpels, and kissed her, with evident pleasure, on each cheek. Middy exclaimed, "It is so good to see you. I thought you were never coming back to work. Tell me, what have you been doing?"

Arpels fought off every instinct to get the meeting over with as quickly as possible. With as much calm as she could muster, she replied, "It's wonderful to see you again, Middy. But I want you to know, straight away, that I'm not coming back. I am near a breakdown and life seems to have lost its meaning. I'm going to take a long rest from the business so that I can find myself again." With that, she sat down.

Middy sat down at her imposing mahogany desk and stared in disbelief at her star model. A heavy silence came up the suite as the two women struggled to construct a conversation. In some ways the two women resembled each other. Middy was in her late forties, and her slender figure had become a bit richer upon the passage of time. Her hair was sprinkled with gray, giving her an experienced, but not exhausted, air. She had reached that stage in life so comforting to many women: she was attractive to both younger and older men. On the other hand, Anne was blonde and in her early twenties. Her body, strong and almost statuesque, possessed outrageous curves and her shapely legs seemed to have been designed, not to reach the ground, but to reach the sky. She was a classic type of American beauty seen so often in the women in Texas, a package that seemed almost irresistible. But these gifts, as always in life, carried a heavy burden. Anne had found, early in her teens, that her beauty attracted both sexes. This had become her secret burden. The principal similarity between the two women was that each gave an impression of discipline and control.

Middy decided to break the impasse. "Anne," she said, "I hope you know and understand what you are doing. At this moment I am negotiating with Coca-Cola's people to make a deal worth millions to the agency in which you will be promoted as the modern American Sportswoman. We have already discussed several skits in the series. In one, you are to portray a modern Amelia Earhart jetting everywhere about the globe. For example, you fly into the Kalahari Desert and land amidst the last surviving group of Bushmen. You are accompanied by an experienced guide who has conducted safaris in the Kalahari Desert for many years. The guide speaks and understands the primitive dialect of the tribe. He points out a distant dark cloud on the horizon and tells you that the tribesmen are about to run toward this cloud as fast as they can, hoping that it is a rain cloud. The cloud appears to be at least ten miles away, and you are amazed at their predicament as the tribesmen tell your guide that there has been no rain for weeks. You ask the guide to tell the tribe to wait; you go to the rear of the plane and break out several cases of Coke, which you distribute to the thirsty Bushmen. Their thirst quenched, they break out in a beautiful ritual tribal dance to their rain god and tell the guide that they want you to become their queen."

Continuing, Middy said, "In another you are assigned to fly your plane over the Himalayas and to land in Tibet in order to introduce Coke to the people. While flying over the tallest mountain peak, your plane has engine trouble and you are forced to land on a high Himalayan plateau. You get out of your plane to assess the damage and see a dim black figure a great distance away. As the figure approaches, it becomes huge and hairy and you recognize it—it is the abominable snowman. In his paw is a huge piece of bear meat, which he offers you. You hand the snowman a Coke, which he drinks with obvious pleasure. The two of you sit down together in the snow and continue your chance picnic.

"There is more," Middy said. "Have you heard about our proposed Saddam Hussein skit?"

"No," replied Anne, her curiosity aroused. "Tell me about it."

Middy continued, "In this skit, you take the part of a present-day Eleanor Roosevelt, possessing beauty, vitality, and intelligence. You are sent to Baghdad as a correspondent for an American-Arab publication. You arrange a chance encounter with Hussein who is captivated by your beauty and charm. A tryst in Constantinople follows, and you have an implied romantic interlude. At dinner one evening, Hussein becomes overcome by both your perfume and appearance and reveals a secret. He intimates that his role in the Middle East is partly that of an 'agent provocateur.' He is acting on behalf of all the Arab oil-exporting nations, and his role is to try to entice American politicians into some cruel military attack against Iraqi civilians so as to swing world public opinion against America. This will always be done when oil prices have gone down to their lowest point in years, thus justifying an embargo when the attack occurs. The net result will be to cause oil prices to rise, which will enrich the Arab oil-producing nations."

Middy continued, "You ask Hussein to open a supposed 'secret weapons factory.' Hussein agrees, provided you spend a week in Baghdad as his guest. In the presence of weapons inspectors from the U.N. and foreign dignitaries from all over the world, a palace is opened revealing a secret computer school for Iraqi women! To great applause, you offer Cokes to everyone present. Anne, you will become the most famous model in the world. Do you want to give that up? Don't forget, there are many beautiful girls in this city who would kill for this assignment?"

Anne looked sadly at her friend. "You know how ambitious I am, Middy. I have worked with you for five years and have done every job you gave me. You also know of my friendship with Kate Cushing. Her death has nearly destroyed me. Middy, I feel sort of dead inside. I can't be beautiful if I don't feel beautiful. I have to recharge and regain some sense of joy in my life." Anne began to weep and silence took over.

Middy knew Anne well. She knew that, behind all that glamour, there was a woman of purpose. She also knew that further argument was useless. In a voice heavy with resignation, she said, "What are you going to do?"

"I'm learning to sail and am going to take a voyage alone," Anne replied.

"What is your destination?" asked Middy.

"To find myself," replied Anne and with that, she left the agency.

Anne returned to her flat, made herself comfortable, and began to assess the changes in her situation. She was out of a job and needed a plan. Anne had never been to university, but she was no fool. She had been raised in a family that insisted upon discussing serious issues during the evening meal. Her father was a professor of linguistics at a university in Savannah, Georgia. Her mother, also in education, was director of admissions and head of curriculum in a private high school, which specialized in the preparation of students for university level work. Her father had remarked upon the practice of creating economic unions throughout the world. He had remarked, during several dinner discussions, that the proposed European common currency, though fraught with both difficulty and the improbability of lasting success, offered an obvious cultural stimulus to peace. For this reason, he had begun research into the creation of a common business language, a modern sort of Esperanto. It was his idea to make such common language compulsory so that, eventually, all commercial and personal transactions within each greater economic union could be simplified.

Anne's mother had insisted upon, and gradually gained acceptance of, the idea that every high school curriculum should require a three-year course in "the great books of history." Her mother believed that educational specialization, taken to extreme, was harmful and hindered the development of what she was fond of calling "the Renaissance mind." She felt that every bright young mind in America should be exposed to at least some of the recorded wisdom of antiquity.

Encouraged by such guardians, Anne participated during her formative years in many discussions, such as "will the universe continue to expand forever?" "Is the so-called 'red shift' theory of Edwin Hubbell caused by the effects by some cosmic mirage as yet unknown?'" "Was Moses a historical person and, if so, why was he the only human being known to have lived seven hundred years?" So, Anne, though as yet unprepared to debate William F. Buckley, had been well taught to assemble all facts bearing upon any problem facing her and to consider all available options before making any important decision.

Anne realized that she was not herself since Kate Cushing died. She felt that something within had died, that some vital organ had switched off. In a word, she felt empty and, what is worse, alone.

Both Anne and Kate had arrived at the agency about the same time. Kate was a year younger, black, full of spirit and fire, with a body sculpted with curves and angles that seemed possible only on a Porsche. They started out rivals but soon became fast friends because they made an unbeatable modeling combination. Every manufacturing company in America was searching for a modeling team of two beautiful women able to pitch a product in clever advertising skits.

They traveled everywhere, stayed together in the best hotels, and became inseparable.

Suddenly, disaster struck. After a brief but agonizing illness, Kate was found to be suffering from an inoperable brain tumor and wilted away. Anne had lost her best friend, dead of cancer at age twenty-one. Since the funeral, she had become inconsolable and floated around the city like a piece of driftwood.

Ultimately, she began to come to terms with herself and decided to enroll at a sailing class given by the Coast Guard at the New York Yacht Club. Her father was an expert sailor who had told here that going to sea was not only an adventure, but a therapy. He had told her many stories of famous people who had found a cure at sea. At his urging, she had read, *Captains Courageous* and Conrad's *Lord Jim.* Both the Coast Guard and her father had recommended a type of schooner made famous by Sir Robert Chicester in his saga, *The Gypsy Moth,* and she soon found such a craft, which she purchased for a song. The schooner had been given an inconsequential, indeed, silly name, which she promptly had changed to *Wind and Water* in honor of a Chinese custom she had grown to admire. The only thing she could remember about the sales transaction was the obvious happiness shown by the former owner in dumping the schooner when the sale concluded.

During all of this period since Kate died, Anne had thought constantly about cancer. Try as she might, she could not understand how this death could happen. Kate had never smoked, had never consumed any alcohol whatsoever, and considered the use of drugs to be an abomination. She knew her body to be her fortune and maintained a meticulous diet. There was no family history of the disease. Anne decided that the current explanations given by the medical profession to be no more than dogma and began a course of self-learning.

She began by reading all available materials at the New York City Library of Medicine (that is, all she could understand). She read the respected scientific journals, such as *Science,* the *New England Journal of Medicine,* the great British medical journal *Lancet,* and the *Harvard School of Medicine Review.* Her interest also turned to holistic medicine and, ultimately, to herbal and plant medicine.

One day, a friend brought her a magazine that contained a review of a book written by one of America's leading botanists. This scientist lived in Virginia and grew many of the plants on his own estate. He had reported that simply chewing the leaves of certain plants would relieve the symptoms of gout and arthritis. What is more important, this researcher had lived in the Amazon forest for several years and said that the Amazon forest was the greatest chemical factory on the planet. He had concluded that most of the plant chemistry within the Amazon forest had never been identified, much less analyzed. It was this botanist's belief that there was a great possibility that plant chemistry existed in that unknown Amazon territory that could either cure or control the twin plagues of our time, cancer and AIDS. The book also contained references to a doctor Bruno Machado of Costa Rica who had found that the poison of a certain green frog had great medicinal qualities.

Anne arranged a correspondence with Dr. Machado and found that one of his special interests was the flora of the Amazon. She also learned that he had built a solid reputation by recording all native herbal or floral medicines of the Amazon that had been proven to be effective. Anne had made her decision. She informed Dr. Machado that she was traveling to Costa Rica and would call him from Colon. She did not mention that she was sailing there, alone, on the

Wind and Water. She feared that the doctor might consider her to be eccentric.

She spent the next several weeks in preparing her schooner for sea. Everyone at the Coast Guard station became aware of her impending voyage. The seamen, the officers, and even the commandant had originally considered her to be a beautiful but silly dilettante who would probably sail out into the Atlantic for a few hundred miles, become frightened, and return to port in a blaze of media publicity. Their skepticism had changed to unanimous admiration, and everyone at the station made sure that her boat was seaworthy.

Anne had made arrangements to have the *Wind and Water* moved to a quiet yacht harbor in Sheepshead Bay. She had carefully studied the harbor charts and saw that it was an easy sail from the Sheepshead Bay to open sea. Both the young sailors and the old coots at the New York Yacht Club had offered to give her a send-off party, and the Coast Guard had offered its cutter as an escort out of New York Harbor. She politely declined because she was seeking, not notoriety, but to reclaim herself.

The day of departure had arrived. She had been advised by the Harbor Master at Sheepshead Bay that she should sail outbound on an ebbing tide, which would nudge her boat seaward. The evening ebb tide signaled to her that the moment of departure had come, and flinging off her bow and stern lines, she took to sea.

Anne, ever feminine, had planned the day of departure (and arrival) well. She had designed and made a nautical outfit consisting of navy blue bellbottom trousers, which fitted so snugly as to demand the sacrifice of underclothing. Her shirt was white, with a Byronesque flowing collar, and buttons that could be opened to the waist. A white sailor hat, worn at a jaunty angle, completed the costume. She was determined to leave New York Harbor, arrive at Colon, Costa Rica, and enter the medical offices of Dr. Machado in this outfit.

Anne was totally unprepared for the commotion that ensued upon her departure. The harbor, which seemed to her to be forever busy, throbbed to the noises and rhythm of ships of every description heading to sea. She decided to keep her boat as far to the right of the outbound channel as possible and used only her foresail so to keep maximum control. She had been told to keep as far away as possible from every ship steaming by so as not to lose control because of the pressure and waves created by the passing vessels. What she had failed to anticipate was that the crew of every merchant vessel and the passengers of every passenger ship stared, waved, and shouted encouragement at her. Every major vessel gave her a spectacular whistle salute. What Anne did not understand was that to the eye of those passing by, she was an impossibly beautiful young woman in a smashing suit who portrayed the marriage of courage with vulnerability. For a brief moment, she thought of herself as an "admiral of the ocean sea."

The standard landmarks of the port slipped slowly astern. The calm of the harbor gave way to the gentle swell of the great sea as the *Wind and Water* drew abreast of that honored marker, the buoy called Ambrose Light. Darkness had fallen; her schooner became at one with the Atlantic and loneliness announced itself as her constant companion. She could only ponder, with no little trepidation, what lay ahead.

V
Rescue at Sea

The first few days at sea did wonders to Anne. She began to experience those calming sensations that seem to affect most people who go to sea. The cloud of mourning over Cushing's death began to lift from her shoulders. Her face took on that blush so becoming to the young; her body began to tingle and glow with the expectancy of the adventure that lay ahead. She noticed that, as every mile was sailed, she felt younger, more alive, and ready for anything.

Anne believed she was well prepared for the voyage. On a chart provided by the Coast Guard, she had drawn a course designed to avoid, if possible, the obstacle of the Gulf Stream current. Since her schooner had sail only, she knew that she must sail south on a course that avoided confrontation with an ocean river that flowed north and east at a speed of about four knots. Therefore, she plotted a general easterly course, which would take her beyond the effects of the Gulf Stream and would then turn right to make the long sail to Dry Tortuga lighthouse at the southerly tip of Florida. Anne would then steer in a roughly westerly direction and sail parallel to and just off the Florida Keys to the lighthouse at Key West. The final leg of the sail would then be a straight course to Colon. The Coast Guard had approved her sailing plan because it avoided the main merchant shipping lanes and the possibility of a night-time collision—the most dangerous situation facing one sailing alone.

At the start of her voyage, the conditions were most favorable except the westerly winds, which blew so lightly her vessel scarcely made headway. The Atlantic, notorious through time as cold and inhospitable, was reasonably warm, and she had settled into a comfortable daily routine. She wore basic clothing; jeans, a warm blouse, and heavy jacket, which made her look rather like a girl on a scouting trip. Her boat, the accommodations of which would seem primitive to many women, was adequate to her needs. It had a tiny "galley" within which she could brew coffee and throw together her spartan meals. The cabin was entirely covered and contained two bunks and a rudimentary toilet flushed by sea water activated by a hand pump. The ship's wheel was in a cockpit in the stern, and the sail locker was forward. Four people would be a crowd on the *Wind and Water.*

Neither the sea nor the handling of the *Wind and Water* had presented a problem. She noticed, almost at the beginning of her voyage, that the design of the hull of her boat seemed to inhibit the possibility of very heavy roll. Each side was fluted outward at the gunwale so that the ship would present greater pressure on the sea to return to even keel. The constantly shifting winds, however, were a daunting challenge. She was constantly forced to tack when facing a headwind and many times had become almost becalmed as she tried to tack about in a light wind. Following winds and sea were likewise a test of her limited experience because she often found herself off course because of the violent sway of the stern. In the main, however, she had concluded that the sea had instantly recognized that she was an amateur and had decided to allow her to make do.

Weeks upon weeks followed as her schooner slowly made its way toward the lighthouse at Dry Tortuga. During this period, she had become a changed person. Every shred of despair had fled, every aspect of self-pity had been exercised, and she began to count the moments until her meeting with Dr. Machado.

Curiously, in these early sailing days of her trip toward Florida, she saw no other vessels. Each day played out in the rhythm of that which preceded it. Her only company was an endless parade of porpoises, which gamboled about the wake of her bow. These fish seemed, to Anne, to be signaling their delight that she had entered their nautical garden. Had she been asked, "Do porpoises talk?", Anne would have said, "They certainly do."

Anne's daily routine at sea had become almost a ritual. She had not learned celestial navigation and plotted the daily noon position of the *Wind and Water* by dead reckoning. Her day began with a salute to the morning sun, which raced from the eastern horizon toward her as if seeking an introduction. An ardent, but unsuccessful, admirer had given her a fine pair of Zeiss binoculars with which she swept the entire horizon. She carefully studied the surface of the sea and determined, by looking at the caps of the waves, from which direction the wind was blowing. She made every effort to determine the action of any current while conceding that it was probably just speculation. At evening, she again swept the entire horizon and then began her meticulous night preparations with which she hoped to cope with the terror of a darkness that seemed, like our universe, to have no boundaries. The first thing she did was to make certain that all night navigational lights were lit. The port and starboard lights, the running lights and a large stern light, were checked and switched on and everything that could possibly come loose in the cabin was lashed down. She then tied the ship's wheel onto the desired course by light but strong twine attached to shackles on the floor of the cockpit. She then laid down a sleeping bag and bedding underneath and directly below the wheel and tied a small string from a spoke on the wheel to her wrist. In this fashion she would be awakened immediately during the night if her boat had, for whatever reason, gotten out of control. Then, she crawled into her sleeping bag and took a series of cat naps until the morning rays of the sun told her the silent night vigil was over.

These early weeks of peace and calm within which no danger whatsoever had appeared had given her the perfect opportunity to come to terms with herself. She sought, and ultimately found, the source of her discontent with both her career and her personal life.

Anne at last realized that Cushing's death was not the main cause of her condition but only a cause. She began to deal with thoughts that her psyche had intentionally suppressed. She began to acknowledge her growing realization that she had not met the right man and had not been able to find intelligent and educated women friends.

As to the men she had met in New York, each and every one seemed not to have learned not to end a sentence with a proposition! Though not understanding why, all the young men she had dated in the city had taken some sort of eternal vow to consider only self. Each male date seemed to take an inordinate interest in sitting only at the most strategic place at a bar (that is, where he was most obvious). Male conversations seemed to take that course set forth in a fortune cookie. Opening gambits always went something like this: "You are the most beautiful woman I have ever met; I have never had difficulty in meeting women in New York (here insert smirk), but nothing like you. Where do you come from (here insert Castor, Pollux, Jupiter or Pluto?) Please stand up, I must see your body. You are a woman who has everything." Anne thought if that is so, how can a person who has everything have nothing? Then such insipid conversation would segue into the obligatory, "What do you do—you look like a model."

Then, within ten minutes of the opening of the conversation, our hero would switch the conversation to, what else, himself.

A particular episode came to Anne's mind. One day about a year or so before a scientist had given a speech in New York about his theory, the Gaia Principle, which had caused a considerable stir among theologians. This professor, named Lovelock, or some such appropriate name, had a wonderfully gentle look about him, a rather tender Einstein. She had heard about his theory, though it seemed to have been met with derision. His theory was simple: the earth is alive; and it brings about, by its own interaction, those forces that create, nurture, and sustain life on earth. Anne was intrigued by the professor's explanation as to how the earth regulates oxygen so that life can be sustained. She also concluded that man's recent moon walk was confirmation of the Lovelock hypothesis. The moon was found to be an inert mass of rock, cold, lifeless, with no enveloping atmosphere with which life could be sustained. Not a single nutrient known to be required for life was present. And yet, this small planet was practically next door to earth!

In Anne's mind, however, the clincher to the professor's theory was his proposed solution. He had noted that the astronauts in their space stations had reported that "rivers of blood" could be clearly seen streaming into the sea from the Island of Madagascar. That island was being rapidly deforested by an ignorant government. He pointed out a condition known to every ecologist of repute: that the great rain forests of Brazil would disappear within one hundred years. Lovelock hoped to make a point to the world that the delicate balance of the earth's atmosphere was in jeopardy. To Anne, his solution took on the majesty of Ecclesiastes. It was that the earth should be festooned with garlands of sunflowers. Thus the earth would be covered by a quilt of flowers, sewn by science, with which to counter the destructive activities of mankind.

Anne had met an aspiring young actor out of Texas named Sam Longshore. He was tall with a lean and sinewy body resembling that of Belafonte. He had mastered a sort of self-deprecatory slouch made famous both by Belafonte and Fred Astaire from which each seemed to spring instantly into frantic but graceful athletic motion. While her mind seemed to have some reservations, her body chemistry sent signals which few women resist. She decided to invite Longshore to a Lovelock lecture and then to have a bite at the Waldorf wine bar.

The lecture was outstanding and upon conclusion brought forth an effusion of appreciation. She noticed that no models or young studs were present. The audience was composed mainly of professional men and women who seemed hypnotized by the brilliance of the speaker's mind. Anne had peeked occasionally at her handsome escort. She noted that his cocker spaniel eyes had glazed over and that his face had taken on a vacant mask. His mind appeared to have fled the lecture hall.

The lecture having concluded, the couple repaired to the Waldorf and ordered a light evening meal. Anne's mind was afire and questions that demanded an answer seemed to generate instantly. Their wine glasses having been duly clinked, Anne began the conversation, determined, at whatever cost, to avoid shop talk.

"What did you think about the lecture?" said Anne. Longshore was prepared to answer, though he knew absolutely nothing about the subject. He was not at all shy about giving his opinion on any subject of conversation.

"Look, Anne," said Longshore, "How can earth be alive when it has no heart and circulatory system?"

"For God's sake, Sam," exclaimed the exasperated Anne, "have you ever seen the General Sherman Redwood in Sequoia Park? It is the oldest living thing on earth and it has no heart. The tree has no plumbing system, but water gets somehow to the top."

Having no answer, Longshore took the usual masculine tack—keep talking and never admit ignorance. Taking a huge gulp out of his wine glass, "And what about his chatter about the regulation of oxygen in the earth's atmosphere," he said. "What difference does it make; there is plenty for all, isn't there?"

The almost primitive simplicity of Longshore's remark infuriated Anne. Fighting to retain control, she said, "The basic idea is that pure oxygen is highly explosive. A single bolt of lightning would ignite the entire earth. If there were no oxygen, nothing could live. How is it that the proper mixture of oxygen, carbon dioxide, and other elements have come about?"

The actor said nothing and ordered another wine. At length he said, somewhat wearily, "Say, do you think Jerry Jones will ever get a good football team in Texas again?" The evening for Anne had ended. She made the usual remarks about facing an "early work day," thanked Longshore for "the pleasure of his company," and never saw him again.

Anne's experiences with women, though dissimilar, also produced disappointment. Upon entering Middlethorpe's stable, she was met with both hostility and fear. She soon became one of the most popular girls in the agency because she never gloated, preened about, or sought to flaunt her mental superiority. Anne had a quality that each model admired and sought out. It was that Anne seemed genuinely interested in solving the problems of others and, in particular, when the problem was a man. Anne had learned, not only from her mother, but from her own life experience, that every woman, however beautiful, needed a man on occasion. Men, she found out, opened not only social but business doors to advancement. She also learned early in life that the mind of a man could be molded as easily as the granite Michaelangelo carved from the hills of the Palatinate. She tried to pass along this wisdom to every girl who sought her counsel. "Don't confront a man; get around a man," was her advice.

Anne's principal difficulty with her model counterparts was that their conversation and interest seemed to be found in only three things, in descending order of importance: (1) personal appearance, loosely described as "image"; (2) "career," whatever that term embraced; and (3) men. Nothing else mattered and no other subjects of conversation ever came up.

A few examples came to her mind. A young Eurasian girl of exceptional beauty came to the city and began to model at the agency. One night she asked Anne over to enjoy a pizza and some wine and to chat. As the pair watched TV while munching on pizza, an athlete came on and announced, "Image is everything." The shy orchid from the Orient turned toward Anne and said, "It sure is."

Whenever any of her friends at the agency suggested getting together, the meeting always seemed to be at some fashion show or similar event attended by the gurus of women's fashion. Not a single model ever suggested a night at the opera, a day trip at the Smithsonian, or a day at the New York Museum of Natural History.

Whenever she went with another girl to the Plaza, Waldorf, or any other popular meeting place, within what seemed to be seconds, young men would wander over to the table upon one pretext or another and the ritualistic mating dance would begin. Anne was tired of, and exhausted by, the entire scene. She desperately wanted to find some inner peace, so that she could find that better path upon which to tread.

And then, suddenly one morning, the tranquility of her southern sail ended. Her morning drill had commenced as usual. She had finished her first cup of coffee and picked up her binoculars to scan the horizon. The morning rays of the sun, in flight from east to west, had, in an instantaneous burst, lit the entire scene. Her binoculars made a full circle and began again in a final sweep. Anne suddenly saw a black spot bobbing upon the surface of the ocean, a few degrees to the right off her starboard bow, and many miles ahead. She put her glasses down, took a strong gulp of coffee, and examined the starboard bow again. There was no doubt about it. An object was floating on the Atlantic.

Anne took to the wheel and sailed directly toward the black object. The wind was so light that her sails scarcely filled, but after several agonizing hours of slow progress, her boat drew alongside the bobbing mass that she now could see was the body of a man, dressed in a black tuxedo, which, in some manner, had become draped over a large wooden crate. At first the scene overwhelmed her; she could not decide what to do. Finally, she remembered the first lesson taught her by the Coast Guard: it is the duty of any mariner to come to the aid of anyone in peril at sea. She brought her frayed nerves under control and began to time the bobbing of the body and the motion of the *Wind and Water*. She reckoned that the only way she could get the man's body into the cockpit was to haul it aboard when the highest point of the body's bobbing motion coincided with the lowest motion of her boat. That point in time at last occurred and with a great heave of her arms, which had grasped the waist of the man, she threw him into the bottom of the schooner. He fell face up in a heap and appeared to be unconscious.

VI
What's Going On?

Anne cast off from the wooden crate, raised sail, and resumed course. She sat in her chair at the wheel and stared at the soggy mess of a man sprawled at her feet. She noticed that his face, though pale and waterlogged, was handsome, that his body was athletic and strong, and that he wore a tuxedo. She could see that he was breathing; his chest heaved beneath the tuxedo jacket and water and frothy bubbles cascaded from his mouth and nostrils. She saw that there was a noticeable bulge beneath the tuxedo jacket and she opened it. A packet of papers, wrapped in a translucent white plastic material, fell to the bottom of the cockpit, and Anne discerned what appeared to be a passport and a considerable bundle of American currency. Anne thought that the man's breathing appeared to be labored, so she stripped off his jacket and shirt. Anne's eyes began a woman's feast. She saw that he had wide, developed shoulders tapering to a small waist; that his pectoral muscles were square and that his abdominals were well defined.

This guy is built, thought Anne and she grasped his chest with both hands and squeezed. With that the man appeared to be coming around, so she stopped caressing his body and looked at her hands. They were trembling! *My God,* she thought, *Am I some sort of necrophiliac?* With that her feminine instincts kicked in and Anne went into a sudden panic. *Look at me,* she thought. *I am dressed in an old pair of jeans and a dirty shirt.* She ducked into the cabin and reappeared wearing the scantiest of red shorts, a light white blouse open to the waist, and a jaunty white sailor hat.

By this time Allenby had come around. His brown eyes now open, he cleared out the last sea water in his mouth and lungs and tried to determine where he was. He smelled the coffee brewing in the tiny galley and in a pathetic, trembling voice asked Anne if he could have some. Without replying, Anne left the wheel, strode into the cabin, and returned with a steaming mug of coffee. The mug had been a gift from a model friend to whom she had given advice about a broken relationship. It bore the ironic legend, "To hell with Men!" A brief silence ensued. Anne kept her lookout straight ahead; Allenby grew stronger as the coffee took hold.

Anne could contain her curiosity no longer, let go of the wheel, and stood directly over Allenby's body. He looked skyward and all he could see was a beautiful face and a pair of shapely alabaster legs. Anne, putting on her game face, and in an attack voice said, "Okay, let's have it; what's going on here?" Anne had reached a tentative conclusion that the mysterious stranger was nothing more than some silly playboy who had fallen overboard during a drunken shipboard party. He was probably one of those attractive but irresponsible gigolos who frequent the Florida yachting scene.

Allenby had not recovered sufficiently to offer an explanation and begged permission from his rescuer to rest a bit. Anne remembered that the previous owner had left some clothing in the sail locker and fetched him a shirt and a pair of sailing pants. He received permission to go below, took off the remainder of his soggy clothing, and returned to the cockpit wearing the abandoned clothing.

Anne let the stranger alone and kept her silent vigil ahead. Allenby sat on the stern sipping his coffee and watched the wash of the schooner ebb away. Each was immersed in private thought and the hours passed. Allenby's color returned; he began to feel himself and felt he owed the lady at the helm an explanation.

Looking right at Anne, Allenby said, "I would like to explain what has happened. I only request that you allow me to completely explain so that I can keep my train of thought. You see, I never thought, a short time ago, that I would ever speak to another human being again." Anne readily agreed, for she too, liked to explain serious or difficult situations without interruption.

He began, "My name is Maxwelton Allenby. I live in California and am a professional person; I am forty-two years old, divorced, and the father of a daughter. About a year or so ago, I began to feel ill; I was not in any pain whatsoever but seemed to be growing weaker. One morning I saw traces of blood in my urine, went to the hospital, and eventually found that I had cancer in two organs and that it had spread to my ribs. I retained the best specialists in the community and received second and third opinions. The diagnosis was unanimous: I had terminal cancer. Of course, I was offered the final solution—chemotherapy coupled with barrages of radiation. This treatment, I was told, would give me perhaps five more years of life. If I did nothing, the prognosis of life expectancy for me was one year. No doctor offered any prospect of a cure."

Allenby continued, "I have had five friends die of cancer, despite going through this prescribed treatment and decided I did not want to end my life that way. I decided to commit suicide by jumping overboard from the passenger ship *Amsterdam* as it approached Miami. When the moment for suicide arrived, I jumped into the sea, but I could not go through with it. My body refused to allow me to do it. I eventually resurfaced, swam for an entire night and on the next morning, nearly dead, found a large vegetable crate floating nearby. I crawled aboard and floated on it for several days. You know the rest."

Anne was struck dumb upon hearing Allenby's story. This water-soaked stranger was grappling with many of the same demons that had been tormenting her! All the radiant joy of Anne's young life had been clouded by the shadow of Kate's death. This stranger's life was drawing to its end from the curse of the same disease. Each sat silently as the schooner glided forward as if on ball bearings.

Then Anne said, "May I say something?"

"Certainly," Allenby replied.

Anne continued, "How do you know that chemotherapy might not bring about remission? Everyone knows that, in some cases, it has been successful in the care and treatment of children."

"That is true,' Allenby said, "but in my case the disease has nearly played out its course."

"What about a spontaneous or miracle remission, if you will?"

Allenby said, "It is too late. I did not want to exit life being killed by a treatment that is supposed to be helping me."

Darkness was approaching. Anne said, "Let's get prepared for the night. I will tell you about myself tomorrow." She set about preparing her vessel for night sail. She decided to continue her regular routine and told Allenby to use a bunk in the cabin. The wind gave an indication that it was freshening, so Anne decided to use only the foresail during the night and went forward and furled the main sail. Allenby offered to take the wheel so that Anne could take a cat nap. Anne declined and said, "I want to get one thing straight right now."

Max replied, "Shoot."

"This is my schooner and I am the captain. Is that understood? I don't want any advice or interference from you and when we make port, I want you on your way."

Max was hurt and countered, "If that is the way you feel, why did you pick me up in the first place?"

Anne had grown a bit weary and snapped, "I don't know. And one more thing," she said, "why would you try to kill yourself while wearing a tuxedo?"

Max turned to enter the cabin and said, "I'll tell you in the morning. You are in a foul mood."

Dawn was breaking. Max had slept poorly and looked it. He saw the galley stove and thought about putting on coffee but decided to wait. The lioness had not yet allowed him into her den. He stepped outside to take a peek at Anne.

Anne opened her eyes and stood up. She looked around and then stretched. Allenby thought, *My God, what a body!*

Anne turned to Allenby and said, "Free the wheel and steer west south west; I will make some coffee." She returned soon with two mugs of coffee and sat near the wheel while Allenby steered. Anne seemed a changed person. The night's rest had restored her; her body seemed relaxed and supple—ready for anything. "All right," she said, "let's hear it. Why the outfit for your death scene?"

Max said, "Fair enough. I will tell you. But first, do you want me to hoist the main sail?"

Anne's eyes widened. *This guy knows nautical terms,* she thought. Looking him over more favorably, she said, "Yes."

The task done, Max returned aft and told his story: "When I told you what had happened yesterday, I didn't mention that I had gone to sea for several years. Frankly, I didn't think it mattered because I felt hardly alive. I sailed on the West Coast, and all the older sailors used to spend time off watch swapping sea tales. It seems that many years ago, around 1850 or so, there were thousands of Chinese laborers who came to California to work on the railroad or in the gold mines. They came to California on the sailing ships with nothing in their pockets and returned home on the sailing ships with what was a lot of money for those times. According to the stories, all the returning Chinese loved to gamble and the voyage sometimes took more than a month. As you can imagine, some of the crew were con artists and many of the coolies lost every dime of the money they had earned in California. The losers did not want to return to their families in China with nothing, so when their ship neared the mainland, they would jump overboard. What made these stories so special to me was that every coolie would put on his best suit before jumping overboard. It seemed as if each thought it best to make a good impression when joining his ancestors. I thought that this was a wonderful custom."

The Caribbean was calm, the winds light, and the schooner seemed to be sailing itself. Tranquility had come aboard and each felt that, within the ambit of what is called mental telepathy, they were drawing closer. The concupiscent Max began to take hope. Several hours of silent sail ensued broken only by Max's request to hear something about Arpels.

"Max, I will tell you why I am out here alone and only ask that you let me set forth my situation without interruption since both of us know we will never meet again once we reach Colon. I will tell you everything if you promise that you will not be judgmental."

"Agreed," said Max, poorly concealing his anticipation.

"My name is Anne Arpels. It is a professional name; I was raised in the Bible Belt of Texas by conservative parents. Both my parents have academic credentials and wanted me to go to university, but I decided to go to New York and try a modeling career. I was eighteen years old, but I felt reasonably well educated. My family insisted that, at every evening meal, serious and meaningful discussions should be held. My mother insisted that television be watched sparingly and required me to read what she called 'great books of history' and to give a brief dissertation on them from time to time. Dad was hoping that I would go into medicine and gave me autobiographies of the life of Pasteur and Madame Curie. He gently suggested that a present-day American hero should be Jonas Salk, not a Tyson. I thought that perhaps this was Dad's way of saying, 'Lend me your ears.'

"I was taken on by a good agency in New York, which wanted to sponsor a new concept of modeling, 'The American Girl.' The concept was simple: find two young girls with the athletic figures popular today to present advertising skits the young people would enjoy. The concept would be the presentation of a modern version of vaudeville, with the product being pushed in clever, but short, skits containing humorous, serious or glamorous situations within which the models would display both talent and beauty.

"I became paired off with a young black girl who was not only beautiful but seemed to move about like an animal. Think, for a moment, of that saucy sprinter from Jamaica. She can run like a deer, win the hundred-meter sprint, and come to the winner's podium looking like she is ready for the cocktail hour at the Plaza. We became the best of friends. Our skits began to take off, and the agency sent us everywhere for presentations and the like. The agency had not hit it big as yet, and we were always booked into hotel rooms with a single bed. One time we flew together to Chicago to work a new routine and after a long day at the studios had dinner and went up to our room.

"We had finished our night preparations and were about to go to bed. I looked into my suitcase and noticed I had forgotten to pack a nightgown. Hoping that Kate had not noticed, I turned off the lights and slipped under the covers. Without saying a word, Kate got up and went into the bathroom. She returned in darkness to bed wearing the most seductive perfume I had ever encountered. She was naked.

"She lay still and my heart began to pound. She uttered a sweet, almost childish sigh, turned toward me and began to massage my breasts. I said nothing and in a flash, she was upon me and her hot mouth found mine and she gave me the sexiest kiss I had ever experienced in my life. Her hands nudged me onto my stomach and, spreading my legs wide, she put her tongue into the deepest reaches of my bottom. She began to pant like an animal, savagely turned me so that we faced and began to suck my breasts. My body felt like it was about to burst. Her head began to move toward the equator. Her lips found my clitoris, and I reached the greatest ecstasy I had ever known. Not a word had been spoken.

"We lay there, panting, like two predators on the Serenghetti. I did not know such physical satisfaction existed in this world. Eventually I calmed and turned toward her and said, 'Kate.' 'Yes darling,' she replied. I said, 'Don't say that word, Kate. Promise me that you will never say anything about this to anyone. Promise me that this will never happen again.' 'I promise,' Kate replied and we fell asleep in each other's arms.

"Our careers were booming and it seemed that every day was better than that which preceded it. We never slept on a single bed again nor was the encounter ever discussed. Our friendship grew stronger as we played out our careers. One day everyone began to notice that Kate did not look well. She constantly complained of headaches and dizziness. We thought that perhaps she needed to have a thorough eye exam, but Kate carried on until she began to display evident balance difficulties during even the most elementary routines. Finally, she took our advice and booked herself

45

into Mayo Clinic. In a short while, we were told that Kate had brain cancer. Within six months she died.

"Max, something was definitely wrong; Kate had perfect health habits. She had never smoked, never used any alcoholic beverages, had never been into the drug scene and watched, with great care, everything she put into her body. She was the only girl at the agency using a nutritionist. She was only twenty when she died. If no external pathological agent had entered her body, how could cancer occur? I began to believe that the disease might well be in us at birth. It began to dawn upon me that the 'cause' of cancer is a chemical or immune system breakdown or perhaps a form of what I call 'cellular mutiny.'

"I began to read upon the subject as my parents had instructed me, and as my study and research progressed, I began to believe that there is a cure out there. You see, Max, there can be no mystery in the universe. Since it was created as an entity, it follows, by the most logical of deductions, that the forces of creation, creating this disease, likewise created its cure. Remember when science first discovered the atom? It was supposed to be the tiniest particle of matter. Then, didn't some scientific geniuses discover subparticles and anti-matter?

"Max, after Kate died, my life seemed to have no purpose. I decided to get out of modeling and to flee the New York scene. I began to have some hope that a cure might be found within plant chemistry. Think of quinine, for example, or Taxol. I had read that the greatest part of the Amazon forest flora had never been discovered, much less chemically analyzed. There is a doctor in San Jose, Costa Rica, who knows a lot about the chemistry of plants, and I decided to sail for Colon and meet with this scientist who also has great interest in the medicine of the indigenous peoples. So, Max, the sum and substance is, this voyage is no holiday. I am

46

trying to find out something about cancer and, along the way, something about myself. Now it is your turn.''

Max decided not to speak for a while. It became apparent that the woman with whom he shared the *Wind and Water* was different from his understanding of that person who had pulled him aboard. A rush of humility came upon him. He realized that he was keeping involuntary company with a woman who possessed the body of Monroe and the mind of a Virginia Woolf. Perhaps an hour passed. The sea said nothing; the wind said nothing. The schooner seemed to be drawn forward by an unknown force.

Anne had, earlier on, asked her companion to use her first name. Allenby did likewise. Their conversations over the past few days had lost any edge, and it was patent that they were moving toward friendship. Max decided to conduct a friendly examination of Arpels. A limitless ocean appeared to lie ahead, and this would give each something to think about. ''Why did you decide to sail this boat from New York to Costa Rica?'' he said. ''This is a dangerous sail, you know, and you could have flown there in three hours.''

Anne was irritated at this question. She felt that Max seemed to have missed the grandeur of her plan. Instantly, she shot back, in a somewhat haughty voice, ''Well, if I had flown, you would be history!''

Recognizing the evident truth of Anne's reply, Max said, ''Touché.''

Anne continued, ''I wanted to sail the *Wind and Water* to Costa Rica to see if I had the stuff to do it; I wanted to meet the plant doctor with a mind cleared of depression and despair and to be ready to do anything or go any place this scientist might suggest. Don't you understand, Max? I needed a catharsis.'' At last, the two minds had met upon a level field. The path to mutual understanding was revealed.

The days passed like those calendar scenes in a movie. Both Anne and Max knew instinctively that each did not require chit chat. There is only so much to say about a modeling career. Max knew that he couldn't continue to keep harping on his insane decision to kill himself. Anne had set out the routine at sea. Max was to clean the ship, to set the sails, and to bail out the cockpit, if the boat shipped water. Anne was the captain.

Eventually Anne decided upon a plan to pass time at sea based on some routines done at home by her parents. She decided that each day when time and conditions permitted, they would discuss a particular important subject. Anne would pick a subject for a day, such as "Is the universe expanding?" Max would then pick his subject. The rules laid down by Anne called for an entire day to think upon the chosen subject. The rules further called for no ridicule, sarcasm, interruption, and, most important of all, no arguments ad personam. Max agreed to commence the discussion.

VII

An Expanding Universe

Max decided he would start with a discussion of "An Expanding Universe." Attempting to imitate Disraeli, he said, "There is a serious question before us. That question is, 'Is the universe expanding?' Anne, I don't know much about cosmology except to say that the present theories about its composition seem difficult to accept. Let me raise some questions and give you some thoughts and impressions. Perhaps this will stimulate conversation and an exchange of ideas."

Anne replied, "Neither do I, but when you finish I have a couple of ideas for discussion."

Max continued, "I believe that the Big Bang Theory might (indeed, probably does) explain the creation of our Solar System but is inadequate when used to explain the creation of what we call 'the universe.' I suggest that the Big Bang Theory is nothing more than a cosmological oxymoron. I say this because its very definition as to how the universe was created is flawed. The universe was created by a 'Big Bang,' the theory tells us. This theory would do justice to the writings of Lewis Carroll; it has a wonderful sense of *Alice in Wonderland* about it. If the universe was created by a Big Bang, it necessarily follows that before the Big Bang, there was nothing. Where were the materials, the mass and energy, out of and from which the explosion occurred? We know that our Solar System was created by some sort of explosion, so logic compels a conclusion that before the Solar

System was created there was some sort of kind of 'universe' containing physical mass and energy. This compels a conclusion that there have been, and will be in the future, many Big Bangs.

"The state of our knowledge of the cosmos is so limited and fragmentary that science cannot even calculate its boundaries. Indeed, theories are floating about today that the universe is limitless and will expand forever. If the universe is constantly expanding, and at an increasing rate of speed, how can we still see stars and galaxies discovered by Galileo five hundred years ago? Can our telescopes see to infinity?

"The word 'universe' is misleading when one attempts to contemplate the construction of the cosmos because it presupposes there is only one 'universe'," said Max. "I suggest that a more correct word to attempt to explain the constitution of the cosmos would be the word 'multiverse,' or possibly 'omniverse.' The multiverse is that enveloping circle of accretions created by a series of Big Bangs. Our Solar System was created by one Big Bang and will end when the sun flames out.

"The physical properties of outer space are as yet unknown to us," Max continued. "For example, how can a ray (or particle) of sunlight, possessing no discernible mass whatsoever, travel from the Sun to Earth without losing momentum? And how can sunlight escape from the gravitational force of the sun? My thought is that the disciplines of physics and mathematics have not evolved sufficiently to deal with problems concerning the universe. The present laws of physics and mathematics work when dealing with problems concerning the Earth. It remains to be determined whether these laws will hold up when applied to cosmological events."

"So consider this," said Max. "Cosmologists state that they are unable to find more than 90 percent of the matter that must be in the universe in order for its balance to be maintained. They further agree that 70 percent of the energy is missing as well. But could not this missing matter and energy be in the cosmic detritus (neutrinos and other sub-atomic particles) that was created by the Big Bang and that melds or joins together with other unknown particles at the edge of the universe to create and replace mass and energy disbursed by the Big Bang? Can it be this distant mass and energy that have kept the universe in balance?

"For example, the theory that the universe is 'expanding' and that it will expand forever is based upon one law of physics, 'the Red Shift.' This theory, proposed by Edwin Hubbell, is now accepted as gospel though no space vehicle has ever been sent out to the edge of our known universe (or even to Jupiter) to determine whether stars or galaxies are, in fact, speeding away from our Solar System. And how do we know that stars or galaxies beyond our Solar System, if moving, are moving in a straight line away from our Solar System? These celestial formations could be moving in a circular direction around our Solar System in an orbit as yet undiscovered."

Max carried on. "Moreover, the Hubbellian 'Red Shift' could be a cosmological mirage, an illusion created by light traveling from celestial objects beyond our Solar System interacting with minute particles of energy or matter, such as neutrinos, or matter contained in solar winds. The illusion of motion in an expanding universe could be created by objects moving in outer space (beyond the solar system), which were placed into motion by other 'Big Bangs' in the multiverse. Everyone has seen a mirage when driving in desert country on a hot day. Haven't you noticed that as you approach a mirage you are absolutely certain that there is water in a depression on the highway ahead of you? But haven't you also noticed that as you draw closer to the 'water' it disappears only to appear again farther up the highway? You have seen water that disappears as your car moves closer! The same idea can be applied to all those 'lights' we see in outer space. Could not these 'billions and billions' of stars (to quote astronomer Carl Sagan) be mirages; that is, the last remnants of light that has traveled to the Earth from now vanished stars? Let me explain what I mean. Let us suppose that an astronomer locates a new star in the cosmos that is calculated to be, for example, on thousand light years away from the Earth. The light that this astronomer saw left that star one thousand light years ago. Does it necessarily follow that this star is still in the cosmos? It could have self-destructed or have imploded into a black hole.''

Max's argument took a new tack. ''Many astronomers and cosmologists of today argue that not only is the universe 'expanding' but that it will expand forever. This implies a limitless universe. An entity (universe) without boundaries is an entity without order. Therefore, these scientists are arguing that the universe is in a state of perpetual chaos.

''Now let's consider this point,'' said Max. '' 'Distant galaxies are flying away at faster and faster speeds' is the current dogma. These exploding stars called supernova are said to be speeding away from our galaxy because they appear to be dimmer than they should be, therefore they are farther away. Perhaps these supernova appear dimmer because they are in that part of the cosmos that contains massive quantities of cosmic dust or detritus, which I argue is the missing mass and energy that scientists claim they cannot locate. These exploding stars could also be the recycling of mass and energy created in the aftermath of the Big Bang. In other words, these distant supernova are continuations of the creative force of the Big Bang. And why have not the cosmologists of today offered an explanation as to why the Solar System is in order if the edge of the universe (or that part of the cosmos beyond our solar system) is speeding away from our galaxy and at a constantly increasing rate?

"There is demonstrable order in our solar system. Ask anyone who has ever taken a *star sight,* or fixed the position of his ship in the middle of the ocean. Celestial navigation works and has proven to be reliable since mankind began its first observations of the stars. Why hasn't the Sun flown off into infinity, leaving the Earth cold and alone? The answer is that there is an order we call gravity, which keeps our Solar System intact. So, too, is there an order keeping our multiverse intact. Finding this 'order' is the task of cosmology.

"Anne," Max continued, "Think for a moment about what Stephen Hawking and other leading scientists say. Hawking says that 'everywhere one looks, the universe appears to be the same.' Whoa! Look at our universe at night, Professor Hawking! Hawking writes that Einstein's Theory of Relativity and the Theory of Quantum Mechanics are irreconcilable. He says if one theory is incorrect, the other theory is wrong.

"This observation of Hawking's would seem to support my argument that the state of our knowledge of space physics and space mathematics is insufficient to understand the true composition of the universe.

"Let's consider Einstein's theory that 'space-time' is curved," continued Max. "How do we know that to be true? Has anyone ever measured or seen such a phenomena? If the universe is 'limitless' and has never had either a beginning nor an ending, then the concept of time, cosmologically speaking, is irrelevant. Time is just a human invention. I believe that NASA should send a space vehicle to Jupiter not just to take pictures of Jupiter but to examine and photograph distant stars and galaxies to determine whether the 'Red Shift' theory is applicable to outer space. And what could cause space to be curved at the outer edges of space where there is nothing there to exert any gravitational force upon space? If 'space-time' is curved, then one may be entitled to conclude that the multiverse is held together at its outer edges by physical properties as yet undiscovered.

"So, Anne," Max finished, "let me suggest that the multiverse that I comprehend can be visualized as a sort of Olympics symbol—circles joined together. Or think of the construction of a beehive. Our Solar System, created by one 'Big Bang' is a tiny part of the multiverse. The multiverse, in turn, is held together by a girdle of creation, as yet unknown or even comprehended by us. I think that this 'girdle' is a celestial cummerbund made up of accretions of subatomic particles created by the consecutive Big Bangs that have occurred throughout eternity. In some manner, these particles have bound together in the cosmos to create a glue that binds the multiverse into an order."

Anne took her turn. "This is my input," she said. "I think that some scientists in this field are undisciplined and present theories to the public that either are unproven or, in some cases, pure speculation. This is done for purposes of grabbing publicity because, as these scientists well know, there are so few people who know or understand their ideas, there is little chance of refutation. Here is an example: some scientist announced recently that 'a star had been found which is older than the universe.' Okay, then so much for the Big Bang Theory. How can something be 'older' than the moment of creation? And, if this scientist's theory is correct, why don't the scientists announce the repudiation of the Big Bang Theory?

"Here is another example: recently it was announced that 'in the year 2015, there is a huge asteroid in the cosmos that could strike the earth.' Then, about two or three days later, an announcement was made that 'we have recalculated our observations of the movement of this asteroid and now conclude there is no chance of this occurring.' What really makes me mad is that about a week later (quite by coincidence, I'm sure), a movie studio announced that a movie would soon be out on this very subject! It makes one wonder about the integrity of science."

Anne continued, "We are taught that 'nothing moves faster than the speed of light.' This is a cornerstone assumption upon which Einstein based his Theory of Relativity. But can we be sure that this is true in outer space where there are no inhibiting gravitational forces? Why could the speed of light not be measured by space vehicles sent out as far as possible into outer space (such as is occurring now with the Jupiter Mission)? My final point is, if outer space is in a state of eternal chaos, why does mathematics work? Mathematics presupposes order. There must be order for any system of mathematics to work. Therefore, everything we know about our Solar System and Earth argues against a universe that expands forever."

The discussion ended. Max and Anne looked at each other and gently smiled. At least their universes were moving closer. Max steered while Anne threw a bite of dinner together. Max felt alive again. Secretly, he wished that the trip would never end.

VIII
Egypt and the Legend of Atlantis

The next day was Anne's turn. She was pleased to learn that Max had studied ancient Egypt and had become fascinated with Plato's account of Atlantis. This is Anne's view of ancient Egypt and its possible connection with the Atlantis legend.

She began, "My family became interested in Egypt by accident. We went to church services every Sunday and on one Sunday, after services, I asked Dad, 'Why do we say 'amen' after each prayer or hymn? What does it add to the services?' I was about sixteen at the time, and Dad said he would look into it from the perspective of a linguist.

"He discovered that the word 'amen' had found its way into the lexicon of Greek and Hebrew and that it meant the same thing in both languages. He then read *The History of Egypt* by Breasted, considered a classic study of Egypt, and noted that those four letters A-M-E-N seemed to appear everywhere in the culture and history of Egypt. Many of the Pharaohs who ruled between the twelfth and eighteenth dynasties had names containing the letters of A-M-E-N or A-M-O-N. He discovered that a local god of Thebes had become the state god of Egypt, the Sun god Amon. He discovered that the name of a great Egyptian Pharaoh, Amenhotep, means 'Amon rests.' Dad concluded 'amen' was either a corruption of Amon or that the two were interchangeable with the other. He then discovered that the history of Egypt recorded the existence of Egyptian 'Hymns to the Sun' wherein the high priests would recite these hymns at religious gatherings. Dad concluded that the Egyptian worshipers at these festivals would rise and shout, or chant, in unison, 'Amon, Amon, Amon.' The response, of course, was to indicate obeisance to their god, Amon, and thus the mantra amen was born.

"Dad then made this observation: every Christian, by saying amen after a hymn or prayer, is worshiping a long-forgotten Egyptian God—Amon. He thought that some theologian might well conclude that this was a violation of one of Christianity's Ten Commandments. 'Thou shalt not worship any other god but me.'

"We divided up our study of Egypt as follows: Mother would provide all the bibliographies and studies that she thought pertinent; I would study similarities between Egyptian and other cultures; and Dad would use his linguistic background to explore such cultural similarities in religion, language, architecture, philosophy, etc." said Anne.

"As a family study team, we made these findings and conclusions," said Anne. "The cultures of ancient China and ancient Egypt are remarkably similar and linked together many thousands of years ago. We believe that the legend of Atlantis provides a clue as to where that link occurred: in the Middle Americas. It is our view that an advanced group of Oriental people crossed over the Bering Strait land bridge and migrated southward until they found their Shangri-La, Meso-America. These people brought with them, not only the culture of ancient China, but great skills in stone masonry, building, and mathematics. We believe that these are the ancestors of those people who eventually formed the early American civilizations of the Olmecs, Aztecs, and Mayans. We consider these people to be "advanced" because the civilizations they developed in Meso-America were technologically far superior to those found in

North America or around the Amazon Basin area in South America.

"Both the North American Indian and the Indian tribes in the Amazon remained primitive hunter-gatherers while the Oriental peoples who settled in Meso-America developed a highly advanced technological civilization. We believe that the first contact between the culture of Egypt and the culture of Meso-America people occurred in prehistoric times and was instituted by voyages of exploration in a westerly direction by the early prehistoric Egyptian people. The Egyptians were a sea-faring people whose civilization was created upon the shores of the Mediterranean Sea. Herodotus wrote in his histories that the Egyptians set out on voyages of exploration thousands of years earlier to find the southern-most tip of Africa—the Cape of Good Hope. If one considers the possibility of good weather and fair winds for a reasonable period, even a crude sailing vessel could sail from the Egypt to Central America in forty to fifty days."

Max raised his hand (the agreed sign for seeking a clarification.) "Anne" Max said, "what do you mean by your words 'prehistoric times'?"

Anne answered, "I mean that period of time between the end of the last Ice Age and the discovery of writing. From what we are taught by the geologists, the last Ice Age ended approximately ten to eleven thousand years ago. Archaeologists have recently discovered evidence that hieroglyphic writing started in Egypt approximately five thousand years ago. My term 'prehistoric times' means that period between eleven thousand years ago and five thousand years ago, a period in which human cultural activity surely took place. But no written record of such activity or cultural connections was made because of the fact that humanity had not yet discovered some form of writing by which such activity could be preserved."

"I understand," replied Max.

Anne then continued on with her discussion of Egypt and Atlantis. "This voyage is intimated in the Atlantis legend. How else could the priests in ancient Egypt have learned of such an 'island west of the Pillars of Hercules' unless told of this discovery by their own navigators? It is from this scenario just presented to you, Max, that we drew the conclusion that Egyptian explorers returned home with the secrets and skills of this advanced civilization in the Americas and used this acquired wisdom with which to build their civilization.

"We suggest that it is possible that the pre-dynastic Egyptian explorers returned home to Egypt with Oriental craftsmen from Meso-America so that these craftsmen could teach the Egyptians the art of pyramid building, stone masonry and working with gold. This interchange of culture between Meso-America and Egypt could have gone on for hundreds, indeed, thousands of years, in prehistoric times. Now, consider the similarities between ancient Chinese and Egyptian cultures. The greatest astonishment is the art of pyramid building in ancient times. On the planet pyramids of antiquity are found only in Egypt and Meso-America. A few pyramidal structures of primitive form are found in Mesopotamia that are copies of those built in Egypt. The Egyptians were a Semitic people, but consider the remarkable fact that nowhere in the neighboring Semitic countries, (Saudi Arabia, Yemen, Iraq, Iran, Kuwait, United Arab Republics, etc.) can pyramids be found. Does this not lead to the reasonable conclusion that the Egyptians developed their pyramid building technology from a people or cultural group extraneous to their culture?

"Now, notice the remarkably similar (indeed, almost exact) construction of the pyramids in Egypt and those in

Meso-America. The pyramid of the Magician at Uxmal (Mexico) has sides of angle of inclination of which is almost exactly that of the pyramid of Chephren (Egypt). The step pyramid near Mexico City is nearly identical in shape to the terraced pyramid at Sakkara (Egypt). The pyramid at Sakkara is said to be the first Egyptian pyramid. It was built to provide 'a staircase to the sky so that pharaoh could ascend to heaven.' It appears that the pyramids in Egypt were built to provide a vehicle to immortality."

"The pyramids in Meso-America, unlike the pyramids in Egypt, were not intended as burial sites but were constructed as platforms allowing their priests to get nearer to the stars. This is why their places of worship were placed at the top of the pyramidal structure. I recently heard that an ancient pyramid was found at Teotihuacan that may be at least 7,000 years old. This has not as yet been verified. If so, this would mean that the pyramid at Teotihuacan is far older than the earliest known Egyptian pyramid (Sakkara).

"The pyramid of Snefru at Medum is identical in shape to the watchtowers which the ancient Chinese spaced along the Silk Road. Notice the shape of ancient temples and pagodas in China. Each floor steps in as the building rises until it almost comes to a point at its apex. We suggest that this architectural style was the ancestor of the pyramidal shape of the Egyptian tomb builders. Now consider the form of the tomb that preceded the Egyptian pyramids. They are called Mastabas in Egypt and are curved, dome-shaped earthen structures. These types of curved-dome shaped burial mounds are found all over both Meso-America and also in North America (Ohio)."

Anne continued, "What about the obvious similarity in the craftsmanship displayed in Egyptian and Meso-American gold artifacts? When one examines the gold artifacts found in the tomb of Tutankhamen with those gold artifacts found in Meso America, one finds the same exquisite workmanship, which would lead one to believe that the artifacts were constructed by machines.

"If one examines the casing blocks at the base of the Great Pyramid at Giseh, it can be seen they are so finely cut the joints are nearly invisible. This advanced craftsmanship in stone is also found in all of the pyramids and large buildings constructed in Meso-America. In fact, the foundation stones of many of the early buildings constructed by the Olmec or other early Oriental people were so well fitted that the Spaniards, in tearing down the buildings, would build their churches upon the foundations built by the ancient peoples! Consider also the stone masonry of Macchu Picchu. Many experts, upon examining this Inca fortress, have noted that a razor blade cannot be placed between the exquisitely set stones.

"Now, what about agricultural methods? Notice that the agricultural methods employed in Meso-America seem nearly identical to those employed in ancient Egypt. Small plots of terraced land, constantly refreshed by cleverly designed irrigation systems, allowed a large population to be sustained by use of a small amount of land. Maize has been cultivated in Meso-America for over 5,000 years.

"When Dad began to examine the writing and habits of the Egyptians, he warmed up to the subject. He set up a picture of the 'Palermo Stone,' said to display the earliest of Egyptian hieroglyphs, alongside a large display of ancient Chinese calligraphy. Chinese characters are written within a form of a vertical rectangle; it is the same with Egyptian hieroglyphs. Each form of writing is a pictograph; a Chinese character and an Egyptian hieroglyph can display not one thought or idea but a multiplicity of things. Each form of writing presented a puzzle, created and used by a special, privileged class of people. Each form of writing appears to have been intended for use by a privileged class; each was created to make an intrusion by a foreign culture almost impossible. Notice that the 'puzzle' of Egyptian hieroglyphs was not solved until the Rosetta Stone was deciphered. Even the Egyptians do not claim to have invented hieroglyphics! Note that primitive pictographs in stone are found in Palenque, in Meso-America.''

"Now let's examine some cultural similarities, all the while keeping in mind that Egypt and China were separated by thousands of miles in an age wherein a journey of fifty miles was an arduous undertaking. Each culture engaged in ancestor worship; each culture honored the concept of filial piety; each was reclusive and guarded its borders and culture from foreign intrusion. Each culture kept itself apart from the rest of humanity. Breasted noted that Egyptian courts were 'Oriental,' with harems and a huge bureaucracy to serve the king. Finally, we noted that the Egyptian calendar and the calendar of the peoples of Meso-America were not only similar but were based on astronomical calculations. The people of Central America had a calendar that went back hundreds of thousands of years. These people believed that time had no beginning.''

Concluding, Anne said, "How does one account for the fact that there are statues all over Meso-America of people with obviously Negroid features? There were no indigenous Negroid people in ancient Meso-America. The only possible explanation is that early Egyptian explorers had Negro people with them when they made their voyages of exploration to Central America. It is also possible that the early Meso-American people who went to Egypt when the explorers returned home could have seen Negro people in Egypt and carved stone images of these people upon returning home.''

It was Max's turn. He offered these observations upon modern explanations of the Atlantis legend: "I have read several articles on Schliemann's discovery of ancient Troy and many accounts by other scholars who insist on placing Atlantis within the confines of the Mediterranean. In fact there is one European scholar who insists that Troy is Atlantis although the physical geography of that Troy discovered by Schliemann cannot possibly square with Plato's account. The hill in southwestern Asiatic Turkey was never low enough to be a Mediterranean seaport; Schliemann's Troy is an area consisting of approximately two football fields; Plato's Atlantis described a 'great city, with a great seaport, with canals entering into and out of the city into a great ocean'; Plato's Atlantis was described as west of 'the Gates of Hercules,' which we now call the Straits of Gilbraltar and on a great island larger than Asia Minor and Libya combined.

"Schliemann's supposed Troy is so small a parcel of land as to make it impossible that a powerful nation was created there. I don't believe that Schliemann discovered Troy, but the limitations of archaeological knowledge of that time enabled Schliemann to convince a number of people that his theory was correct. Based on our present knowledge of geology, archaeology, and cultural anthropology, the most logical spot on our planet that matches Plato's account of Atlantis is Central America. Moreover, the geography and physical characteristics of Central America (particularly around Mexico City and the Yucatan Peninsula and that area near Mexico City where the ancient city of Teotihuacan was built) closely match Plato's description of Atlantis 'as a vast island, larger than Libya and Asia put together, with mountain ranges and lush plains and earth rich with precious metals.' "

Max pressed on, "I believe a valid argument can be made that Teotihuacan could be the source of the Atlantis

legend. Archaeological examination and evaluation of Teotihuacan and, indeed, the whole area of Meso-America, is just
beginning and the experts who are at work in this area say
over ninety percent of Teotihuacan is still buried. It is said
to be the first city of the Americas and that portion of the
city that has been uncovered shows that it was constructed
with great skill according to a precise urban plan. It contains
a giant pyramid—the Pyramid of the Sun—and archaeological evidence recently uncovered indicates that Teotihuacan
was a hive of industry giving rise to extensive trade throughout Middle America. The Aztecs called Teotihuacan 'the
City of the Gods' and considered it to have been built by
'great craftsmen' (the Toltecs). Present archaeological evidence indicates that the city has been rebuilt many times
and that it could have been occupied by an even earlier
civilization—that of the Olmecs. The Olmecs are known to
have been master builders and sculptors. Consider their
work in obsidian, their massive stone heads and the Olmec
Rain Baby, which sculpture records both Asiatic and Afri-
can features.

"I also want to make another point about the geography
of the area," Max said. "Plato made it clear that, according
to the legend told by the priests of Egypt, Atlantis lay at the
center of a vast island. Teotihuacan is toward the center of
that portion of Central America near what is now known as
Mexico City. There could have been an ancient port
city—let us say around Vera Cruz—which served as the port
for Teotihuacan, giving rise to all of the maritime activity
ascribed to the city known as Atlantis. The ancients could
well have thought that Meso-America was a 'vast island.' "

Max continued, "I don't believe that Plato's account of
Atlantis should be taken as the literal truth. But Plato was
one of history's first great scientists. I suggest that he recorded the Atlantis legend in his dialogues not only to present a morality tale but to preserve forever the account of the

Egyptian priests so that future civilizations could consider it for what it was worth. Plato is considered one of mankind's first great thinkers, philosophers and scientists. Indeed, the knowledge of mankind for the first 1,000 years of its history owes a great deal to Plato. Plato did not invent the Atlantis legend, but he preserved it. I believe that there was a historical place on the planet that Plato chose to name Atlantis. Plato wanted to preserve for antiquity the fact that nine thousand years ago there was a connection between ancient Egypt and a certain people he called the Atlanteans. I believe that this ancient cultural connection happened and that the connection was between a great early civilization that developed in Meso America and Egypt and that the people of Meso America taught the pre-dynastic people of Egypt the art of stone masonry, which eventually led to the construction of the pyramids of Egypt.

"Anne, let me make two other points about my theory of a connection between Meso America and Egypt, which may have occurred around ten thousand years or so ago. I refer to the so-called 'mystery of the Sphinx.'

" 'The mystery of the Sphinx' concerns its antiquity. For many years the standard explanation of the construction of the Sphinx was that it was ordered by a pharaoh named Chephren and was built around 4,500 years ago around the time of the construction of the second Egyptian pyramid. Scholars in Egypt, to this day, insist that this is the fact and argue that the face of the Sphinx is that of Chephren. However, recent studies of the structure indicate that the Sphinx is far older than earlier believed and that it was built before Egypt became a desert. The Sphinx is now being restored and studies indicate from weathering patterns and earlier repairs to the structure that the Sphinx was built at a time when there was no civilization or technology in Egypt capable of accomplishing such a feat. There was no civilization or technology in Egypt seven thousand years ago! All scholars and experts upon Egypt agree on this point. It is my belief that the Sphinx was built by artisans and stone masons from Meso America who were the only people on earth possessing the skill and technology in stone masonry to construct such a monumental project in stone at that early time in the history of mankind. The age of the Sphinx ties in with the Atlantis legend. The people of Meso America had the skills and know-how to construct, from a solid block of stone, a figure in Egypt that was meant to represent an early Man-Beast God.''

Anne replied, ''How do you know that perhaps the opposite voyage occurred? Couldn't it be possible that prehistoric Meso American people made the voyage of discovery eastward to Egypt?''

Max answered, ''That could be the case. But there is no written or historical evidence of it. The people of Meso America were not a seafaring people. There is no evidence that the civilizations of Meso America traveled even to the islands of the Caribbean, much less across the Atlantic.''

Anne had another point to make. ''Isn't it possible that the Oriental influence upon the culture of Egypt occurred because of an east to west flow across land? In other words, could not the Oriental influence have traveled to Egypt in antiquity along the Silk Road?''

''Again, yes,'' said Max. ''But keep in mind that both civilizations kept the most meticulous records known in antiquity and there is no mention of such a cultural interchange.''

Max concluded by making this observation: ''Insofar as archaeological research is concerned, archaeology in Meso America is in its infancy. Archaeological research has been conducted everywhere in Egypt and the Middle East. Little attention has been paid so far to ancient civilizations in Meso

America. When the areas around Teotihuacan, the Yucatan Peninsula, and Central America have been thoroughly explored, if pyramids are found that are older than found in Egypt and a city near the Caribbean is uncovered with features approaching Plato's account of Atlantis, my theory may gain acceptance. We already know that, in Teotihuacan, there are pyramids and great public buildings larger than those in Egypt. We know that there are more than one hundred thousand pyramids in Mexico yet to be explored.''

Max made his final point. ''As of now, very little is known of the earliest of the Central American prehistoric civilizations—the Olmecs. One hundred years ago, the Olmec civilization was unknown. We do not know exactly when their civilization started nor do we know when or why it ended. Very little attention to this civilization has been paid by the archaeologists of today. However, within the past thirty or so years, ancient relics of the Olmec civilization have been discovered quite by accident. These relics are giant stone heads over eight feet tall situated on stone pedestals. These Olmec heads are estimated to weigh more than fourteen tons and display excellent skills in ancient stone masonry. They have been uncovered in uninhabited jungle growth areas in the Central Mexican states of Tabsco and Vera Cruz in that part of Central American Mexico that is near the Caribbean Sea.

''Think about this point for a moment, Anne. Where on the planet, in prehistoric times, are found giant stone buildings or structures created with great skills by prehistoric stone masons? The answer is, (1) on Easter Island; (2) in Central America; and (3) in Egypt. Now, we must ask, is there a cultural or anthropological connection, and if so, what is that connection? I believe there is such a connection; that all such prehistoric stone masonry was done either directly by Asiatic peoples or by people trained or influenced by Asiatic culture or skills. The Easter Island giant stone statues and the pyramids, buildings, and stone heads of Central America were created directly by Asiatic people; the pyramids and great buildings and figures of ancient Egypt were constructed by technology that the ancient Egyptians borrowed from the prehistoric Central American Asiatic people. In a word, the prehistoric Asiatic people were the Michaelangelos of stone masonry.''

Anne had one more point to make. ''Max, Plato's legend of Atlantis refers to a period in time eleven thousand years ago. How do we know that Asiatic peoples were in the Americas that long ago?''

Max replied, ''We do know that Asians inhabited the Americas more than eleven thousand years ago. Scientists recently tested the bones of a woman that were found on the Channel Islands off California forty years ago. DNA tests and an analysis of the amino acid of bones revealed their age to be thirteen thousand years, far older than any previous hominid bones found in North America. This finding proves that the earliest inhabitants of North America pre-date the Atlantis legend by two thousand years. A civilization capable of creating an 'Atlantis' could well be developed within a geological period of two thousand years.''

An entire day of sailing had passed peacefully, and the sun began to seek its respite. Max reached toward Anne and grasped her hand. ''That was a wonderful presentation,'' he said.

To her surprise, Anne felt Max's hand to be most reassuring. She reluctantly withdrew and said, ''I'll fix a bite; you keep a lookout for a while.''

IX

The Storm

The voyage of the *Wind and Water* continued on. The schooner had passed the lighthouse at Key West and Anne had changed course toward Colon. The wind was fair and the seas calm, and both sailors had settled into a pleasant, if unspoken, routine. Anne gave the orders when needed and did most of the steering. Max kept the vessel clean and shipshape. Max said nothing about his experience as a sailor or that he had been a licensed Merchant Marine officer. He honored Anne's early order "not to stick his nose into the operation of the *Wind and Water*."

Max had decided to get up every morning at least one hour before Anne so that he could look over the schooner and also make those early morning observations so helpful and necessary to a sailor. One morning, just before dawn, he thoroughly examined the boat to be certain that it was still completely seaworthy. He checked the forward sail and gear locker, the cabin, the scuppers, and the mast and rigging. Everything was in order. Dawn began to break and soon the horizon cleared revealing a vista of incomparable beauty. The sea was as calm as a sheet of glass; a light, perfumed Caribbean breeze scarcely filled the fore sail; the air was warm and serenity abounded. Max wondered what conditions could exist that would cause the poet Goethe to write, "Nothing is more difficult to bear than a succession of fair days."

What a sourpuss, thought Max. Max knew, all the same, that Goethe was no seafarer.

Max and Anne continued their daily mind games. One day Anne chose "women in the military." Her idea was that women and men should serve in separate military units. Max had selected a commentary on "the failure of the American jury system in criminal cases." However, a few days later, peace and tranquility aboard the *Wind and War* came to an end.

The first indication that a change in the weather was about to begin occurred when Max awoke one morning and took his first inspection tour about the schooner. Dawn was breaking and he could both see and feel that the westerly wind was freshening. The fore sail had filled (the main sail was not used during the night sail), and the ship's rigging began a gentle whine. Then the sun began to rise, and he could see that the Caribbean Sea was capping everywhere. Each wave began to crest into a white foam, and a swell began its build-up. The swell began to take effect upon the *Wind and Water,* and as the sun rose higher in the sky, he saw the first clear sign of danger known to every experienced sailor—the morning sky was everywhere bright red. Max recited to himself an old sailor's quatrain:

Red sky at night,
Sailor's delight;
Red sky at morning,
Sailor take warning.

Anne awoke, left the wheel, and went into the cabin to make coffee and freshen up. Max took the wheel. She soon returned and the pair exchanged customary early morning small talk. Max said nothing about the weather and waited to hear Anne's comments on the changing sea. Hours passed and the *Wind and Water* began to pitch up and down, and the gathering westerly swells began to pound with great thuds against the sides of the schooner. Sheets of spray began to fly into the cockpit, and the scuppers made a sucking sound as water rushed out of the cabin floor. Then, a perceptible change took place. The clouds had grown thicker and heavier as each hour passed, and now the sky began to darken as the wind began to howl. Anne did her best to sound like an experienced mariner. She said, "The weather is turning bad."

Max replied, "I will take a look at the barometer," and he ducked below. Max quickly returned to the wheel and told Anne that the barometer had fallen rapidly.

Anne, who had never faced such a situation before, said, "What do you think?" For the first time in her sailing career Anne was worried.

Max replied, "We are headed into a storm."

Within four hours the message was clear: a giant Caribbean storm was brewing. The sky had turned black, the barometer continued to fall, the wind was howling fiercely, and the sea began to form great rolling swells that crashed against the schooner's hull. The schooner's bow began to swing violently from port to starboard and back, and with each rolling motion, it seemed as if the vessel would capsize. Anne began to lose control of the wheel; the motions of the schooner became more violent and she was frightened. She turned to Max and said, "I'm afraid, Max. I can't keep the schooner headed into the seas. What shall we do?"

Max replied, "You told me at the outset to keep my nose out of it; didn't you?"

"For God's sake, Max, I'm sorry," Anne shot back, "but this is no time to sulk. Help me!"

"All right," said Max. "We must take all necessary steps to prepare for the worst. We must lower the fore sail, tie everything down on the schooner, and prepare to bail out the cabin when we begin to ship water. Most important of all, we must put out a sea anchor. Do you have a sea anchor?''

Anne replied, "What is a sea anchor?''

Max answered, "It is a large conical-shaped canvas bag open at one end. There is an iron ring at the open end attached to a harness, which is tied to a long, strong manila rope. It is always kept in a chest that should be marked, 'sea anchor.' ''

Anne said, "There is a locker on the starboard side of the cabin by the bunk. I use it to store some personal things."

Max realized now that Anne was a novice; he knew that Anne had never faced any grave danger at sea. He hurried below as the seas began to become more powerful and angry. He found the locker and opened it. It was full of Anne's underwear! *My God!* he thought, *The Coast Guard lets anyone go to sea these days!* He threw her things on her bunk and presently saw the stencil, "sea anchor." He hauled the equipment out of the locker and returned on deck with the sea anchor.

Max knew that the time had come for him to take over if they were to survive the storm. "Anne," he yelled, "Keep her nose into the seas if you can, while I go forward to stow the fore sail. I will tie the sea anchor to the bow so we can try to ride out the storm." Dragging the sea anchor behind him, he worked his way to the fore sail and furled it as the mounting seas crashed over the bow and drenched him to the skin. The wind howled and the rigging was singing at high pitch. Dragging the sea anchor with him, he made his way to the pitching bow where a large iron ring lay and tied one end of the long manila line to the ring. He then threw the sea anchor overboard and gently let out the line until it was taut; the sea anchor took hold. He then returned to the wheel where Anne stood, her face ashen, a look of utter terror upon her face. She was absolutely drenched and totally crestfallen. "I will take over now," said Max, as he took the wheel from Anne. "You crouch down in the cabin and bail out as the water floods in. I'm going to try to keep the schooner headed toward the west so that it will face quartering seas. The main idea is to avoid being capsized by seas that meet us athwartships." A grateful Anne let go the helm and slid to the cabin floor where she grabbed Max's legs. The battle for survival had begun.

The sea anchor had taken full hold, and the bow of the schooner faced the onslaught of the storm. The wind seemed at hurricane force; it was midnight and the little schooner fought for its life in total darkness. By now, the storm appeared to be at fever pitch; great waves crashed against the bow, causing the schooner to shudder like a wet dog. It pitched up and down in violent motion as waves of water cascaded from the bow into the cockpit, flooding the scuppers. Anne bailed frantically as Max tried to keep the schooner facing at a forty-five degree angle to the onrushing seas. Hours passed as Max fought to keep the vessel from capsizing. Every time the schooner swerved violently to port or to starboard, the faithful sea anchor would gradually pull the bow back into position ready to meet the next onslaught. Great streams of sea water and flying spray cascaded onto Max and Anne as their battle for life continued. Anne continued to bail and neither said a word as each tried to confront the terror of the storm.

The greatest danger they faced during the night was the ever-present possibility of capsizing. Every once in a while, a great wave would throw the schooner either to port or to starboard, exposing the entire side of the vessel to the next oncoming wave. This would cause the *Wind and Water* to make a frightful roll. On these occasions, Anne would scream in terror and yell, "Max, we are going to roll over!" but each time the vessel somehow righted itself and labored on.

Max would yell over the screaming wind, "Keep bailing; the sea anchor is holding. We will make it." As each peered out into the darkness, nothing could be seen. The schooner and its occupants were alone.

The long night of the storm continued on as the two sailors battled for their lives. Max and the sea anchor kept the schooner headed into the heavy seas as each prayed that the storm would end. Max looked to the east and saw the first glimmer of morning. Then, as quickly as it began, the storm showed its first sign of abating. The howling winds began to die down, and Max let out an exultant yell, "The storm is letting up. We are saved!" Within moments the wind died down and the great waves of the storm began to lessen. Within two hours, most of the storm had passed and the *Wind and Water* was bobbing upon a calming sea as the faithful sea anchor kept its bow in position. Max and Anne had won.

Anne stood up and looked into Max's tired eyes. Both were drenched, worn out, and the schooner was a mess. All sense of authority had fled Anne's demeanor. She looked like a frightened woman who wanted desperately to be held tight. "Max," she said, "you have saved my life. You are the captain now. Take me; I'm yours."

"Anne," Max replied, "I can't; I'm impotent. The medicines, you know, I have been taking to treat my cancer."

"Then eat me," shot back Anne.

"Anne, I am an attorney, solicitor, proctor, counselor, advocate at law!"

"All the more reason," said Anne, determined to get a relationship started.

"Let's wait until we get to Colon," Max replied, at last. "I'm absolutely exhausted. I will pull in the sea anchor, make sail, and we can clean up the cabin and get some rest." The *Wind and Water* resumed its final sail to Colon.

X
Dr. Bruno Machado

More than twenty-four hours had passed since the storm reached its peak. The gale-force westerly winds had stopped and had shifted around to a gentle following wind. No white caps could be seen and everywhere one looked, all was calm. The air was warm and scented; it had taken on a sort of shimmering aspect. Both Max and Anne were at peace, which neither had experienced for more than a year.

Max had taken over all responsibilities of sailing the *Wind and Water*, for which Anne was grateful. She fussed about the cabin preparing for landfall. Max had to rely upon dead reckoning because of the schooner's compass and radio direction finder had failed during the storm. The force of the storm had pushed the schooner eastward many miles. Max reckoned that the schooner would pick up the light of the Colon lighthouse early next morning and advised Anne to keep a lookout on the starboard bow for the signal. The two sailors spent a quiet night at sea in their customary routines as their schooner made its way to the east coast of Central America.

Darkness was still upon the sea as Max awoke. He was determined to keep a sharp lookout while Anne rested because he felt certain that the lighthouse would soon be raised. Max was right. The first rays of morning sun made a timid appearance as Max spotted the alternating red and white pulse of the Colon lighthouse. Dawn broke with typical

Caribbean brilliance, and within an hour's sail, the coast line of Costa Rica could be seen. Max figured that within four hours they would be safe within the harbor. As the schooner drew closer to shore, all kinds of activities could be seen. Fishing boats were going in and out; a variety of shipping was entering and exiting. At length, their boat drew abreast of the lighthouse and the long passage from New York was over.

Anne had considered celebrating their arrival at Colon by opening one of the few bottles of wine that she had carried aboard for ceremonial occasions. She thought the better of it, however. She would wait for just the right moment. Anne had never felt happier; never more expectant. She eagerly awaited the next adventure. Max said nothing. He placed his right hand into hers and gave it a long, warm squeeze, which said everything. He wondered whether this mystical encounter was ending.

The *Wind and Water* was now safely in port. The harbor master's launch approached and asked the usual identification questions. The officer in charge spoke excellent English and showed them the way to the yacht club of Colon. The schooner was safely docked and secured for a long stay. The harbor master was most courteous and took them to the Customs office where clearance was made. The Customs officers became quite curious upon finding out that Max had no baggage and that his passport and money seemed partly water-logged, but eventually they attributed the situation to the "crazy habits" of these "Americanos del Norte." The harbor master told the couple that the best hotel in town was the Grand Hotel Maria Isabella, and after Anne got packed, they set off for a few days in Colon.

The Maria Isabella was indeed grand. It was located in the center of Colon on a huge piece of ground that contained an ornate garden fronting the hotel. The hotel was on that massive scale one sees on the famous "Croisette" in Cannes. They climbed up a huge entrance that led to a massive lobby and an ornate registration desk. A tall, formal-looking clerk in severe dress approached, and Max asked for a large room for two with a single bed. The clerk demanded to see their passports and noticing that the couple were not married, he suggested a suite of adjoining, but separate, bedrooms. Agreement being promptly reached, Max and Anne were led to their suite accompanied by a bellhop carrying Anne's two suitcases. The bellhop departed and the couple passionately kissed. They were on land at last! They were in civilization again! Anne said, "Max, the first thing I'm going to do is take a long bath. I want to relax and freshen up before calling Dr. Machado."

"Great idea," Max replied. "I have to call my daughter to let her know what happened. I will get money transferred to San Jose and can hardly wait to get into a tub myself."

Max had finished first and lay on his bed, fully clothed, waiting to take Anne to an early dinner in the hotel dining room. He could not believe his good fortune. He felt that he had been reborn; his body was full of strength and energy; all of the dread trappings of his disease had left him. He desperately hoped that his time with Anne was not ending. Max was ready for anything.

The door to the bedroom opened, and Anne stood before him, dressed in a transparent black negligee. Max had never seen her looking so fresh, so youthful. Her eyes were dreamy and she said nothing. Max sprang into action. He moved toward her like a snake about to strike and put his arms around her waist; Anne began to shiver. He gently lifted her up and placed her on the bed. He then removed her negligee as though it was a wrapper on a candy bar. Her beautiful, alabaster body awaited. Max undressed and lay beside her. He moved his head toward the inverted triangle and gently blew on her pubic hairs. They waved to and fro like grass on a hillside. For an insane moment he thought of General Custer. He gently placed his body up on hers and began to massage her breasts while their mouths met in a fierce embrace. He then lifted her up a bit and placed a pillow beneath her bottom so that he could kiss her clitoris in every imaginable way. Anne began to moan with joy and screamed that she was at climax. Then a wonderment occurred. His penis—dormant these many months as he fought the disease—became rock hard, indeed insolent, as if it had assumed a separate existence. Bursting with newfound aggression he said to himself, *Thank you, old soldier, for returning to duty,* and introduced it into Anne's white-hot body.

The next day they decided to make the necessary preparations for meeting Dr. Machado. Max went off to get a suit and some appropriate clothing. Anne made arrangements to have the *Wind and Water* sailed back to New York. The harbor master had found two young sailors who were willing to do it for a reasonable sum. Max and Anne would fly back to New York when the adventure ended. They had a late lunch in town, rented a car, and were ready to take off for San Jose.

The next morning arrived, and they checked out the hotel and began a leisurely drive up the main highway that linked Colon to San Jose. The concierge at their hotel in Colon had suggested a slow drive, pointing out that there was much to observe along the constantly changing scenery. The four-lane highway was lined with trees, and the concierge had told them that they could see many three-toed sloths along the way, and perhaps they might spot a harpy eagle. However, the concierge said that chance of spotting the legendary quetzal bird was slim. He was right. They never saw one.

Their day ended with a late afternoon arrival in San Jose when they checked into the Cariari Hotel in the outskirts of the capital, San Jose. This hotel was tastefully decorated in an Oriental style and had every possible amenity, including gambling. They had a quiet evening about the hotel and looked forward to their meeting of tomorrow.

At precisely ten o'clock on the following morning, they arrived at the Institute of Plant Research and were shown to Dr. Machado's office. Max had dressed in a fashionable black suit of Italian cut, which he had purchased in Colon and Anne had chosen her sailor suit outfit with which she had commenced her voyage.

The receptionist showed Anne into the doctor's office. Max insisted that she go in alone; this was to be her show. She entered a large, somewhat cluttered office and saw a young man with black hair slouched in his chair reading what appeared to be a racing form. He was casually dressed and was wearing slippers. No white coat for this specialist! "Hello," said Anne. "I am Anne Arpels from New York."

The young doctor stood up and said, with a look of astonishment, "You are the woman with whom I have been corresponding?" It was obvious that Dr. Machado had never imagined such a lovely person would be appearing in his office.

"I am," said Anne, "and I am most anxious to speak to you. I have brought a friend with me. May I asks him in?"

"Yes," replied the doctor. "Excuse me a moment; I will be right back."

Anne also left, going out to get Max and reentered the doctor's office. Max took a look at the periodical on the doctor's desk and confirmed it contained data concerning the day's entries at the Hippodrome San Jose. The doctor returned, having changed into a very stylish black suit and appropriate shoes.

"Will you have coffee?" the doctor said. Both Anne and Max said yes and coffee was brought in and the trio began conversation. "I am Dr. Machado and received my medical training in Spain and the United States," he said. "My specialty in biology and the chemistry of plants. It is my hope to aid my country's agriculture by reducing or eliminating plant diseases. Costa Rica earns a lot of dollars exporting coffee, bananas, and the like. Because of this, I have also studied the plant chemistry of the Amazon Forest. I know of your general interest, Miss Arpels. Can you be a bit more specific?"

"Yes," said Anne. "Doctor, I hope to interest you in doing some research on the possibility of finding some chemical or toxin produced in the Amazon that might offer hope of a cancer cure. You surely are aware of the recent discoveries regarding Taxol, which is derived from the bark of the yew tree. My research has found that much of the plant chemistry of the Amazon Forest is unknown. Isn't it possible that a new quinine, applicable to cancer, might exist in this forest? Or, could there be a medicine, discovered by the indigenous people of the Amazon Forest, which might help?"

"I anticipated as much and have discussed this with my colleagues," said Dr. Machado. "There is such possibility, but I have not looked into as yet because there are, as yet, some serious problems presented."

"What are the problems?" asked Anne.

Dr. Machado replied, "There have been continuing rumors and unverified stories about a lost tribe of Waorani Indians called the Tageiries who live in a part of the Amazon Forest in Peru. This area is east of the Andes in a region known as the 'Oriente' where are found the headwaters of the Amazon. This tribe has never been contacted as yet by white people because of their reputation for ferocity and their widespread practice of homicide. I have heard these stories during my travels to Manaus where I consult with Brazilian experts on the flora of the Amazon Basin at the Institute. In Manaus there is a large group of another primitive Indian group called the Yannomammi. The Brazilian government has been conducting a social experiment by which the government hopes to 'civilize' these indigenous peoples.

"These Yannomammi live together in a settlement located in the outskirts of Manaus, and there I met an old shaman of the tribe who told me about the Waorani, who are feared by all Indian tribes. This shaman told me about a legend that says many thousands of years ago the Waorani, who originally lived in the Brazilian Amazon forest, split into two separate groups, the Waorani (the people) and the Tageiris. The Tageiris evolved into the fiercest and most feared of the Waorani people and migrated west and north to the 'Oriente' where they found a hidden valley never visited by a white man. Their reputation for ferocity was such that other native Indian tribes in the 'Oriente' left them alone, and they soon established a large territory to the south of the Napo River, which they control to this day. They are still a savage people; a few years ago they killed five young American missionaries who had flown a small airplane into their territory. It is told that this lost tribe chose this hidden valley because the chief of the Tageiris, and his shaman, wanted to create a superior race of warriors. The conflict that had been created amongst the Waorani people was that the shaman of the lost tribe believed that the secret of creating a superior warrior lay in the selection of a certain preferred female, not male!

"Now the problem is that neither I nor the government of Costa Rica have the finances to support an expedition to this remote area in Peru. Moreover, none of the local Waorani tribesmen who are not Tageiris would help me in this expedition because they fear the Tageiris who have killed many of their neighbors. I have learned to speak a little Waorani and also speak Quichua and know how to get near the fringes of this hidden valley, but I would have to go there alone.

"Let me get to the point. The significance of all of this is that within this hidden valley is a large area where all disease is said to be unknown! The shaman says that he has been told that huge vegetables like broccoli and cauliflower grow in this area, which manufactures very strong chemicals. The shaman was told that there are no weeds of any kind growing around these giant crucifiers and that local animals never bother these plants, which appear to be immune to any disease. It is told that these plants are ground into a pulp to which is added an extract obtained from the bark of a strong local tree. The bark is said to contain very potent chemicals manufactured by the tree in its defense against insects. The mixture is then eaten in a tribal ceremony presided over by a shaman. This mixture is reputed to have miraculous healing and preventative powers. It is eaten to stimulate the body's own immune system. I would like to analyze the chemical properties of this medicine and also to physically examine any Tageiri said to be cured by it. The shaman also told me that it is told that no children of this Tageiri Tribe ever die of any type of 'wasting disease;' in fact, wasting disease is unknown to the Tageiris' medicine men."

Anne interrupted, "We have money. Would you consider an expedition with us?"

The doctor replied, "I have a suggestion. There is much more to tell you about the Waorani. You should know the risks before considering such an expedition. Let's have dinner tonight at my club. I will tell you more of what I know about these Tageiris and their customs. Dinner at eight at the Turf Club de Costa Rica. Agreed?'' Max and Anne readily accepted the invitation. Dr. Machao agreed to pick them up at their hotel.

The trio arrived at the Turf Club promptly at eight and were ushered into a private dining room by the host. It was quite obvious that Dr. Machado was well-liked at this club. The Turf Club sat on the bluff of a high hill overlooking San Jose. The club had once been the home of a coffee planter, and the grounds of the estate had been converted into a race track. In the background, piano and guitar music could be heard mingling with the sound of animated conversation. The atmosphere was elegant, and Anne, in particular, was thrilled with the prospects of dining out with such a stimulating companion as Dr. Machado.

The party was seated, cocktails promptly arrived, and dinner was quickly chosen. Everyone was animated and Dr. Macho seemed to almost be presiding over a medical conference. He said, ''Let me tell you about everything else I have heard of the Waorani legend, and then I will present a sort of general plan for you to review. When I am through, I would like to hear something from you two as to what is going on in American politics today. Please, no decisions tonight. I insist that you think over my proposal.'' Max and Anne indicated agreement and the doctor continued his discussion.

''In order to know more about the Waorani and to better understand this legend told to me in Manaus, I went to Iquitos in Peru where I eventually located a shaman of a more peaceful group of the Waoranis,'' he began. ''I was told that the Waorani were never a large group of people. They are said to be descendants of a small group of Asiatic people who, many thousands of years ago wandered south from North America, crossed the Central American land bridge and ended up in the northwestern part of the Amazon rain forest. In stature, they are small with short legs, which seem out of proportion to their robust trunk. They are a strong, agile people who are hunter-gatherers living off the provenance of the rain forest. They have no written language and their language is unlike any of that of their Indian neighbors. They might well be described, by the standards of modern anthropology, as an aboriginal people and are constantly at war with neighboring tribes. By nature, they are violently homicidal and think nothing of killing another native Indian for little or no reason. In fact, when a member of the Waorani tribe has been killed by an 'outsider,' in revenge the Waorani will kill not only the person who killed a Waorani, but that person's entire family, including his children! All medicine is practiced by a tribal shaman who enjoys a priestlike status. The shaman acts as a sort of repository of tribal knowledge and neither works nor engages in any routine tribal duties.

"According to the shaman I met in Iquitos, the Waorani tribal legend tells of a time in the long ago when the original Waorani tribe split into two separate tribes, each governed by its own chief and shaman. One group insisted upon carrying on an ancient tribal custom, which held that male beauty was critical to both the improvement and survival of the tribe. The strongest and most handsome men became the tribal studs; the homely warriors were mostly ignored. In a word, the handsome men became tribal gods. This custom gave rise to a curious tribal mating ritual. Periodically, all the handsome tribal studs and the young women of the tribe were assembled at a giant sing-song around a great bonfire. Then, the shaman would play an ancient tribal love song on a flute made of bamboo. Each stud was required to sing the love song and those who produced the most faithful and purest rendition of the love song were put into a special, privileged group of tribal studs.''

Anne interjected, ''What is this group called?'' she asked.

''The Kleen Tones,'' replied Dr. Machado.

''Now, what resulted over time in the evolution of the Waoranis was that the tribe using male beauty as its standard for child production created a tribe of dimwits walking around in penis sheaths. The other group (which eventually became known as the Tageiris) was led by a shaman who had achieved stature amongst the tribe not only because of his great intelligence, but because of his healing powers. He had taught them to read both the stars and the sun so as to be able to plant their crops at just the right time of the season. He had also taught the tribe that it was the female of the group, not the male, which made the greater genetic contribution to the tribe. He advised the tribe to use the strongest, most intelligent, and healthy women as child bearers, not the most beautiful. He also recommended that his group move away from the tribe who wanted to breed along the old ways, and this is how the Tageiris migrated into the Oriente where they found their hidden valley. Thus it was that this lost tribe, using female intelligence and health as its breeding standard, evolved over the ages into a fierce tribe totally isolated and safe within the confines of the valley, south of the Napo River in or near Peru. They are reputed to have discovered many cures derived from plants within their territory.

''One more thing. These Waoranis are said to possess great powers of mental telepathy. They seem to know beforehand when an enemy tribe is poised to attack. As the story goes, when a shaman divines that an enemy attack is about to take place, the night before the impending attack, the shaman orders a ceremonial war dance. However, as the warriors assemble to begin the war dance, he instructs each warrior to dance around the fire with his back to the flames instead of facing the flames. In some manner, the shaman has learned over time that the light from the flames, upon striking the back of the knees of the warriors, keeps them alert all night! Then they attack their enemies at five in the morning and catch the enemy warriors asleep.

"They also have another curious custom, Miss Arpels."

"Which is?" replied Anne.

"If you will pardon me, they seem to worship the contours of the female ass," continued Dr. Machado.

Finishing his discourse, the doctor said, "This is my proposed plan. We fly to Iquitos and stay there for a week or so making our preparations for the expedition into Tageiri country. We will rent a helicopter and pilot and take it by boat as far as we can into Waorani country by going upstream on the Napo River, which flows right by Iquitos. We will then fly the rest of the way to the hidden valley. We will locate the plateau or meadow nearby the entrance to the Tageiri territories, land there, and hike into the area where the giant vegetables grow. Now, let's talk about America," he concluded.

Anne and Max remained silent for a few moments, overcome by Dr. Machado's proposal. This was what both had hoped for, a chance to look for a possible cancer cure in the Amazon Basin. Each sipped wine, awaiting the proper moment to change the topic of conversation.

"Thank you for your comments upon the Waorani," said Anne. "We will think it over and let you know soon." Ever feminine, Anne commenced by asking the doctor his opinion on the latest 'episode' in the 'crisis in the White House' concerning Monica Lewinsky, Paula Jones, and Gennifer Flowers.

"You know," answered Dr. Machado, "I admire a man who is well-balanced in life."

"What do you mean?" responded Anne.

"Well," said the doctor, "in a recent deposition taken in the matter, the president admitted that he has taken time to smell the flowers."

Dr. Machado continued, "What is curious to those of us in Central or South America is the double standard that is applied by American women when the subject of adultery is concerned. When a man commits adultery in America, the women consider it to be grounds for divorce, impeachment, or perhaps murder. When a woman commits adultery, the women in America consider this to be 'romantic.' Consider the plot of the recent film, *The Bridges of Madison County*. In this film, a lonely married woman enters into a protracted adulterous relationship with a photographer who happens by. The American women consider this to be a wonderful 'romantic interlude.'"

Max now entered the conversation. "Doctor, Anne and I have discussed the problem created by our American politicians taking large financial contributions from foreign lobbyists or influence peddlers. We consider this practice to be immoral and dangerous to America's future. Do you have any thoughts on this practice?"

"Yes, I do," said Dr. Machado. "We have a great problem with foreign influence peddling in Costa Rica. Much of the wealth of the country is in foreign hands. However, we are a small country. Your problem is far different."

"How so?" countered Max.

"Let's keep names out of the discussion and concentrate on the principle involved," Dr. Machado said. "Remember one of your first presidents who warned the nation against 'foreign entanglements' in his farewell address? I put this case to you. One of the greatest foreign policy dangers facing America today is the problem of how to deal with the situation created when the Republic of China decides to use force to reunify with Taiwan. I believe that this scenario is inevitable because Taiwan is considered to be the so-called 'model of Asian capitalism.' Therefore, its continued existence as a separate nation is a threat to the future of communist China. Moreover, Taiwan remains 'living proof' that capitalism is a better economic system than communism.

"Now, I ask you to assume that when this forced unification situation arises, mainland China possesses full nuclear launching capabilities. This means that any nuclear attack on America's part would be met by an equally effective counterattack by the Chinese. Further, assume that a war between mainland China and Taiwan is impending and that Taiwan asks for American assistance, playing its trump card of campaign contributions to the American political party in power. Is there a person in America who believes that such gifts are made purely in the spirit of friendship? How can an obligated American administration deal honorably in such a situation? Only Mr. Perot and Senator John McCain have had the political and moral courage to speak out against this practice. And this scenario exists elsewhere," the doctor continued. "Look at America's involvement with the problems existing between the Arab and Jewish peoples in the Middle East. America is rapidly becoming the principal enemy of the Arabic peoples."

Dinner ended with an exchange of customary pleasantries, and the party prepared to leave the club. Dr. Machado ended the evening by saying, "I have also heard of a particular place in China where cancer is said to be unknown. It is in the northwestern part of China abutting Tibet. It is called Shambhala. We will talk about it at another time."

XI

The Amazon

Max and Anne decided to stay about the Cariari Hotel for a few days, awaiting Dr. Machado's call. Anne suggested they spend a day around the pool discussing the pros and cons of the doctor's presentation. Max agreed; he knew that neither of them knew anything about the dangers of the Amazon or its inhabitants. He arranged for a breakfast service to be set up poolside and their discussion commenced.

Anne had listened carefully when Dr. Machado said, "This is a dangerous journey."

"Max, do you think we should go into an area so dangerous that it is avoided by the authorities as well as by the neighbors of these Waorani?"

"I do," replied Max, "for if we don't go into this unknown territory, our trip will be worthless. If we go into the Waorani Reserve or Protectorate areas, located in Ecuador, we will learn nothing because this group of Waorani have become somewhat civilized and rely upon modern medicine provided by the government. Moreover, these Waorani tribes trade their wares with hordes of tourists who descend upon them from Quito. These tribes probably never have had any contact with the Tageiris."

"How would we protect ourselves?" asked Anne.

"We will discuss this with Dr. Machado, of course," replied Max, "but we must carry guns for the obvious reason that the area we intend to explore is so far from any help that we have to be able to defend ourselves from any attack.'' He continued, ''Resorting to firearms will be our last defense; I don't want to kill for any reason, but we now know that they have spears, blow-guns, and a sort of machete. We also know that they think nothing of resorting to homicide when their territory is invaded by 'outsiders,' so it seems foolish to rely upon either faith or science to protect us.''

Anne had another point. ''What about our protection while in the jungle?''

''Again,'' said Max, ''we will rely upon Dr. Machado for advice. He is a medical doctor; we can bring along medicines for snake bites, get appropriate vaccinations or medicines for yellow fever and malaria, etc., and wear the best protective clothing available. The only large animal I know of that is dangerous to man is the jaguar and it never attacks a group of people—only the solitary hunter or straggler. We can carry our own water supplies and can get advice from Dr. Machado as to how to adequately protect ourselves from mosquitoes and other insects. Remember, Anne, Dr. Machado has been to the Amazon many times, although not to the area occupied by the Tageiris.''

Dr. Machado called the following day, and told Max that he had ''further information'' and was ready for a meeting at which the group would make its final decision. Ever gracious, Dr. Machado insisted upon taking them to dine again at his club.

That evening promptly at eight, the group gathered at Dr. Machado's private dining room at the club and a delicious evening meal with wine, selected by Dr. Machado with great taste, was consumed. Upon completing the meal, Dr. Machado ordered beakers of brandy to be brought to the table and the serious moment of the dinner conference arrived.

Although Latino to the core, Dr. Machado got right to the point. He had a wonderful flair for gathering one's attention without seeming bossy or overbearing. Gently tapping the edge of a knife on the rim of his brandy glass, he said, "I have come up with some more information about the Amazon and also a plan as to how to get into the Tageiri territory. Have you discussed this trip and are you ready?"

Max took the initiative: "We are ready and eager to hear what you have to say. We have some questions, of course. I am prepared to pay all the costs of the trip if you will guide us and offer your knowledge of the area and your experience. Tell us about your plan."

Dr. Machado continued. "First," he said, "let me say a few words about the geography of the area and the approximate location of the Tagieri tribes, according to the latest information. I have spoken to the authorities on indigenous Indian affairs in both Quito and Iquitos and have learned that these Tagieri tribes continue to migrate in an easterly direction along tributaries of the Amazon. They have no contact with any government agency; all information comes informally from neighboring tribes who fear the Tageiris. In fact, a killing by a Tageiri was reported as recently as 1994.

"As best as can be determined, they seem to inhabit those areas between the Nashino and Cononaco rivers at or near the border of Peru and Ecuador. It is also reported that they have been seen in the area between the Shiripuno and Cuchiyacu rivers in Ecuador. One bit of information remains constant irrespective of its source. The Tageiris do not want to associate with other Waorani tribes and, above all, they don't want to associate with the white man. We can approach the Tageiris from one of two ways. We could start in Quito, Ecuador, and work down by road to Tena and then proceed by boat downstream on the Napo River. We could also approach their territory from the east, starting at Iquitos, Peru, and going upstream on the Napo."

Max interjected, "Which, in your opinion, is the better approach?"

"I favor Iquitos," Machado replied. "Iquitos is the most Amazonian town in Peru and is considered to be the capitol of the Amazon region. It is a port city, and it would be easy to locate a suitable river boat there. Iquitos has an airport, so we could rent a helicopter there and construct a wooden landing pad on the stern of a small tug. Iquitos is on the Amazon, and a few miles downstream, the Napo River flows into the Amazon. We could take the Napo upstream and work westward toward the Tageiri's territory. You might be interested to know that Iquitos is a town of four hundred thousand inhabitants, but it cannot be reached by road. One gets to Iquitos either by air or by boat. By going to Tageiri territory from Iquitos, we can see the most primitive part of the Amazon basin and would have a better chance of locating the Tageiri."

"Agreed," exclaimed Max. "Now, tell us about the general plan."

"My idea," said Dr. Machado, "is to fly to Iquitos and make it our expedition headquarters. The Hotel El Dorado has been recommended by a colleague who lives in Iquitos. Once there, I will take whatever time is needed to rent a medium-sized tug. There is a lot of maritime activity going on in the port of Iquitos. There will be no difficulty in renting a tug and a crew of two sailors. We could then take it to a local shipyard and have a wooden landing platform built over the stern. I can go to the airport at Iquitos and hire a helicopter with pilot that is capable of carrying four persons. I'm convinced the only way of locating this hidden valley of the Tageiris is by helicopter. We will go downstream to the juncture of the Napo and Amazon, go upstream on the Napo to the junction of the Napo and the Cononaco rivers at which point we would be close enough to begin exploration by air."

"Magnificent," Max exclaimed. "This way, we don't have to tramp through the jungle. We can get to the entrance to the hidden valley by water."

"Exactly," replied Dr. Machado. "It would be too dangerous to approach the valley by land. There are no roads and the jungle is almost impossible to get through. That is why the native Indian population use the rivers as a natural highway."

Anne looked concerned, "Doctor," she said, "what about guns? Do we have to bring them with us? I don't want to have anything to do with the killing of an Indian. And how can we communicate with the Tageiri? If they see us armed, won't they think we are about to kill them?"

"This is a good point and I have thought a lot about it," replied the doctor. "I speak Spanish, of course, and some Quichua, which is the lingua franca of the Oriente. I have obtained a brief glossary of Waorani words prepared by a missionary linguist who spent considerable time in the Oriente among the Waorianis. I think I could make myself understood in the Waorani language, but I concede I can find no Waorani word for 'cancer.' I believe that I could make them understand that we are friendly, that we have a shaman with us, and that we are looking for the health tree. One other thing. If I can, I hope to bring a westernized Waorani with us as an interpreter. I think one can be found in Iquitos. As for guns, they are absolutely necessary."

Doctor Machado then addressed Max. "Are you prepared the meet the costs of this trip?"

"I am," said Max. "Can you give me a range of the costs plus your fee for acting as our guide and instructor?"

"I want nothing for my services," replied the doctor. "I estimate all costs should not exceed two hundred thousand dollars."

"Agreed," said Max, and the two men shook hands.

The doctor concluded, "Come to my office tomorrow and I will arrange for you to have all the necessary shots. I can also tell you what type of clothing and footwear to buy while I make arrangements for our flight to Lima and transfer to Iquitos. We should be ready to leave in about ten days. And, Anne, be sure to get a St. Christopher's medal." Dr. Machado enjoyed teasing Anne.

Dinner had ended. Dr. Machado took Max and Anne back to the Cariari. The journey was about to begin.

In due course, all preliminary preparations for the trip were completed and the trio flew into Iquitos, the capitol of Peru's largest department, the Loreto. It was within the confines of the Loreto that Dr. Machado hoped to contact the Tageiri. Clearing customs, they went directly to the Hotel El Dorado, which was located within two blocks of the Amazon River. The hotel fronted on the Plaza de Armas and was in the center of a bustling jungle town that once was the center of a thriving rubber industry. The small hotel proved to be a fine recommendation, and upon checking into their rooms, the group began preparation for the voyage up the Napo River.

Dr. Machado felt that his first task was to locate an adequate tug, which could accommodate a helicopter, so he took off for the waterfront. He suggested that Max and Anne have a look about the city and shop for the clothing and equipment needed for the trip. It was decided that they would regroup at the hotel at 7:00 P.M. and dine at the Don Giovanni, an Italian restaurant nearby. Dr. Machado recommended a leisurely walk along the Raimondi, a street running through the center of Iquitos which also heads to the Belen market area.

Max and Anne were excited as they walked hand in hand through town. Never in his wildest dreams had Max thought that he would be in the Amazon with a beautiful young woman. The buildings and stores along the Raimondi and Melecon were in sharp contrast. Some were neat, well-maintained, and fronted with bright blue Portuguese tile. Others were shabby and decrepit, looking like slum dwellings. Everywhere motorcycles and curious vehicles that looked like motorized rickshaws sped about. The young men of the city stared in astonishment at Anne's beauty, but they kept a respectful distance as Max guided her about. The day sped by. They soon found everything needed for their jungle trip and spent the bulk of the day shopping. Anne poked around several shops where great quantities of Indian crafts were displayed and found one that had objects made of animal bones. Max found a beautiful blowgun, but he decided to wait a bit before purchasing it. One young man who spoke English pointed out the "Iron House," which was very near their hotel. It was said to have been designed by Gustav Eiffel. Max thought it looked like a collection of scrap metal and suspected it was a "joke" perpetuated upon the "Gringos." Their first day was a huge success.

Eventually, the group met for dinner as planned. Dr. Machado was full of enthusiasm. "I have found the perfect boat for our trip," he said. "It is a medium-sized river tug which has been used to move large barges around the port. I spoke to the captain, who is a young German who speaks excellent English. He has an assistant and is agreeable to allowing a temporary wooden platform to be built over the stern. He says the tug can make eight to ten knots and has an excellent diesel engine. He is willing to go upstream on the Napo to approach the territory of the Tageiri people, but he says he won't go into the jungle. He offered to anchor his tug in any river of our choice and suggested we equip the group with a radio. He has heard rumors about the Tageiris around Iquitos for years and considers them to be very dangerous. He told me where to go in the port to have the platform built and wants fifty thousand dollars for the rental of the tug and his time. The only other thing the German pointed out was that he had never heard of, or taken any tourists into, the area I described. He believes that this part of the Oriente is, as yet, unexplored by the white man."

Max said, "Doctor, that is agreeable. You finalize the deal tomorrow. I have already transferred money to a bank in Iquitos." The remainder of the dinner was spent in recounting their shopping experiences in the city.

This procedure was followed for many days. Dr. Machado bore the main responsibility for the preparations necessary to enter Tageiri territory. Dr. Machado was more the gracious host than a guide. He knew that, in addition to preparing the tug for the voyage, the location and renting of a helicopter would take time. Moreover, official approval was necessary from the Peruvian authorities, and the doctor wanted time to contact local Indian people in order to have all the information possible about the Tageiri and where they might be found. He well knew that this part of the Oriente was largely unexplored, even by the government of Peru. Knowing he would be occupied for perhaps two weeks, he provided a list of places to see and things to do in the area about Iquitos.

Dr. Machado had recommended a day visit to Lake Quistacocha where a boat could be rented for a paddle around the lake. He also pointed out to Max and Anne that there was a zoo at the lake containing many local animals and also a fish hatchery. Anne had a luncheon basket prepared at the hotel, and the pair took off in a motorcarro for the lake, which was a short distance from the city. The zoo contained jaguars, ocelots, and agoutis. Anne shuddered when she saw a giant anaconda about twenty feet long slithering about its cage. An attendant threw a live agouti into the cage; Anne turned away. She couldn't stand the sight of that great snake wrapping itself around an animal no larger than a medium-sized dog. They were shown the fish hatchery where a giant primitive fish about six feet long swam slowly in circles about the tank. It had a huge, thick body and a head similar to a catfish. The native people called it the Paiche. The attendant said it weighed more than three hundred pounds and was a fruit eater. Neither Max nor Anne had ever heard of a frugivorous fish. The attendant explained that this had come about as a consequence of the annual flooding of the river banks by the Amazon. When the Amazon floods, it permits these fish to swim to the base of the fruit-bearing trees that line the banks of the river. When the fruit falls, the giant Paiche have a feast.

The couple spent many happy days poking about the city as Dr. Machado completed the preparations for the voyage. At this suggestion, Max and Anne spent several days about Belen, which could be reached by walking down one of the main streets of Iquitos. The locals refer to this area of Iquitos as the Venice of the Amazon; Max thought the comparison too generous. This area of the port of Iquitos consisted of huts and crude stores built on rafts that floated on the river. Many thousands of local Indians were said to live on these floating houses, which faced a huge market place where all sorts of local medicines could be found. They tasted a delicious rum drink laced with an extract from the bark of a local tree.

Finally, the day came when Dr. Machado had completed all the arrangements. He had arranged a celebration dinner at a local bar and restaurant famous for its music. It was the popular dance club known as the Bamboleo Discoteca. It was said to be frequented by the city's prettiest young women, and it was here that Dr. Machado made his first pass at Anne.

That evening at 9:00 P.M., they arrived at the discotheque and were escorted to their table. Every Peruvian male in the place stared at the tall and voluptuous American beauty who had chosen a skin-tight red dress for the evening, which left nothing, and therefore everything, to the imagination.

Dr. Machado was in high spirits. He ordered a dinner of Peruvian specialties and a fine white wine and brought Max and Anne up to date on his final preparations for the trip. "The tug is prepared to sail," he said. "We have constructed a large wooden platform over the stern with cleats on the deck so that the helicopter can be secured. The tug captain supervised the work and told me that this rig would not impair the operation of the tug in any way. The captain has been advised of the approximate range of our search on the Amazon and has supplied the tug with ample water and fuel. I have rented a four-passenger helicopter and pilot, and it will fly here tomorrow and land on our tug at precisely 1:00 P.M. We will sail out of Iquitos and stream upstream to a wide part of the river about ten miles from Iquitos and circle about until the helicopter arrives. Then we will turn around and head downstream until we reach the fork of the Napo and Amazon rivers. And one more thing," Dr. Machado said, "through my contact with a local Waorani shaman, I have found a young Waorani who is willing to come along to help us find a trace of the Tageiris. He speaks a little English and seems to both speak and understand Spanish well.

"He insisted on only one thing," continued the doctor.

"What is that?" asked Max.

"He insisted on being allowed to leave the Tageiri territory at any time if he felt in fear of his life, and I agreed."

The dinner progressed along; everyone ate and drank ravenously, knowing that this would be the last such occasion for a long time. Both men seemed unable to take their eyes off Anne whose dress looked in danger of bursting its seams. Max's eyes became soft and loving; Dr. Machado's eyes narrowed and his demeanor took on a hungry look.

The dinner having concluded, fresh drinks were brought to the table and furious dancing commenced. The place was packed with young, energetic couples, and the dance music alternated between American dance tunes and wonderfully energetic and melodious Peruvian songs. All evening long the local Peruvian men circled their dance partners near Dr. Machado's table in order to gaze at Anne.

Max was a reasonably good dancer and escorted Anne about the crowded floor with competency. When the wild Peruvian numbers began, Dr. Machado took over and it became immediately clear to Max that his colleague was a superb dancer who appeared to be hypnotized by Anne. Max sucked furiously at his drink, and his face began to flush as Dr. Machado's routines began to draw the attention of all the couples on the floor.

It was during a particularly steamy tango routine that Max's admiration of Dr. Machado's dancing began to turn to rage. Max knew that he had been drinking heavily, but at the same time he thought Dr. Machado's dancing had become offensive. The tango music had grown louder and louder and young bodies appeared to be strung together like spaghetti about the dance floor. During what seemed to be the crescendo of the dance, Dr. Machado had managed to stick one of his legs between Anne's legs so that it pressed tightly against Anne's pelvis as the sensuous music pounded away. Anne's eyes were closed, her cheeks were red, and Dr. Machado's arms were locked about her in an embrace that appeared to be intended to lead her to the nearest motel.

The dance finally ended, and Dr. Machado escorted an agitated Anne back to the table. Max spotted exultation in the doctor's eyes. Max was both pissed and drunk. He stood up, somewhat unsteadily, and said to no one in particular, "I feel kind of woozy. I'm going to wash my face," and he stumbled off to the restroom.

Dr. Machado moved to a chair next to Anne, placed his right hand on Anne's left leg, and squeezed it tightly. He could feel the marvelous muscle tone of Anne's body, and his heart began to pound. He realized, without the slightest feeling of guilt, that his penis had come to full salute.

"Anne," he said, "Max will be gone a while. I want to tell you that I am crazy with love for you and want you to stay with me when we get back to San Jose." It was most obvious that the tango had achieved its desired effect.

Moving her leg away from Machado's grip, Anne replied, "Stop it, Bruno. I am in love with Max. Don't you understand? He didn't have to come with me to the Amazon. We have been together, night and day, and I know what kind of person he is. We are in this together. I never told you this before, but on the sail to Costa Rica, Max saved my life."

Dr. Machado's face clouded, and he replied, "I know that Max is a good man, but, Anne you have to understand something; Max isn't cured. He will probably die in two years. People with this type of cancer never recover."

Anne was upset. "Don't say those things. Just look at Max. Does he look like a dying man to you? We might find a cure. Someone else might find a cure. And above all, he might be in a permanent remission. I intend to stay with Max, if he wants me, as long as he lives. Bruno," Anne concluded, "I am very attracted to you physically. But I'm in love with Max. Promise me that you will be totally professional during our trip—whatever happens. Let's let the future take care of itself." Machado knew that his attempt had

101

failed. He looked at Anne, his Italian eyes sad. "I understand. This won't happen again."

Max returned to the table looking refreshed; his eyes had cleared and his skin no longer flushed. Anne turned quickly to Max and said, "Max, I'm tired. Take me back to the hotel. Doctor, please stay if you wish; we will be ready to leave early tomorrow morning." Defeated, Dr. Machado replied, "I'm coming. Tomorrow will be a busy day."

The next morning they packed for the trip and checked out of the hotel. The hotel permitted them to store clothing and personal effects not needed for the Amazon trip, and they set off in a cab to the tug, which had been renamed the *Bismarck* by its captain.

Arriving dockside, they boarded the *Bismarck* and were introduced to the captain, Karl Krueger, and his deckhand, Ernst Bruening. The tug was a squat, broad, strong-looking craft sporting a new wooden superstructure on its stern. It appeared to be a hundred feet long and twenty feet wide with a wheel house and a small cabin space behind. The group was soon to learn that the tug had no passenger accommodations; passengers had to sleep on deck below the temporary wooden platform. Anne didn't say a word. She was prepared for anything. Max and Anne strode about the deck as Dr. Machado and the captain ran a final inspection. Without saying a word, Max and Anne walked to the stern and threw their luggage on the deck. This was to be their home throughout the forthcoming adventure.

Captain Krueger was a young, tall, broad-shouldered man who spoke excellent English. He was a graduate of Heidelberg University who had decided to "knock about" the world for a few years before settling down. Iquitos was a busy port, and he was pleased to tell his passengers that he was making "good money" as a tugboat captain. He seemed pleasant and told Max and Anne that he was looking forward to going upstream into Waorani country. Bruening was a quiet young man of twenty who was, as he said in passable English, "just seeing the world."

Dr. Machado had concluded his final walk about the *Bismarck* with Captain Krueger. He had received assurances that the tug had received a hull inspection recently and that the diesel engine was in fine condition. The captain pointed out four extra barrels of fuel lashed together behind the cabin area and noted that the water tanks were full. He also noticed two barrels of aviation gasoline securely stowed on deck. By this time, the young Waorani had arrived.

Upon being reassured that all final port clearances had been obtained and that all governmental documents allowing their entry into Waorani territory were on board, Dr. Machado delivered his maps of the territory to the chartroom and the party cast off. In due course, they headed upstream on the Amazon to that point where the river widened and awaited the helicopter. Sharply at 1:00 P.M., they heard the beating sounds of its rotor and the craft landed on the wooden landing platform of the *Bismarck*. The tug turned around and headed downstream. Their voyage had begun.

As soon as the tug had gathered headway, Dr. Machado said to Max and Anne, "I have a surprise. We are going to a biological station located on the river about seven or eight hours sail from here. We will anchor there tonight and spend tomorrow at the station. I hope to get some information on the Tageiris from the director. In any event, it will be an educational stop for all of us. I will tell you about it as we go along." He then turned toward the Waorani Indian who was seated on the gunwale of the tug and motioned for him to come over. He wanted Max and Anne to meet a person who he felt might lead them to the hidden valley where the health tree grew.

A pile of folding canvas chairs lay nearby, and Dr. Machado opened four of them and made a circle, which he hoped would stimulate conversation. The young, slender Waorani Indian approached and Dr. Machado said, "Anne, Max, this is Amö, who is from the Waorani Protectorate in Ecuador." Everyone took a seat and with the doctor acting as interpreter, conversation began. Amö was of medium build, very brown, and appeared to be about twenty-five years old. He had black, coarse hair, large and friendly brown eyes with a face that looked unmistakably Asiatic. He was about five feet six inches tall with slender legs and a powerful upper body. His physique was lean and well-defined.

Dr. Machado spoke to Amö, using a combination of Spanish and Quichua, and the group learned that he came from a Waorani family, which had lived in the Protectorate in Ecuador for many years. He had received some schooling, had been taught a little Spanish, and had decided to come to Iquitos alone to seek a new life. Amö told the group that he wanted to become a guide on the tour boats that sailed the Amazon out of Iquitos and said he would take any employment while he worked on his English and Spanish.

Eventually, Dr. Machado asked Amö if he knew or had heard anything about a group of Waoranis called the "Tageiri." Amö replied that he had never seen a Tageiri, but he had been told by the tribal shaman that they were "wild people" (Aucas) who lived in the jungle between the Nashino and Cononaco Rivers near the border of Peru. Amö said that these wild people considered all other Waoranis to be "outsiders" and that they might be cannibals. Amö also said that the shaman of his people told everyone to stay out of Tageiri territory because they were fierce warriors. Amö also mentioned that the Tageiris used a very powerful poison, curare. The initial conversation with Amö ended and, grabbing his belongings, he went to the stern of the tug to watch the river traffic as the tug made its way down the Amazon toward Explornado Camp where the biological station was located.

Max, Anne, and Dr. Machado remained in their canvas chairs and chatted away as the river scene changed endlessly. Local fishermen in small dugouts could be seen fishing along the banks of the great river. Large cargo ships steamed in midstream, headed either to or from Iquitos, and the afternoon sped by. The steady, rhythmic chug of the diesel engine created a relaxed atmosphere. At this moment in time, even the Spartan conditions of the tug seemed most bearable.

After a few hours of travel, a tall, slender, dark-haired man approached the seated group and took the chair vacated by Amö. He introduced himself as Roberto Fantini, the helicopter pilot hired by Dr. Machado. Fantini appeared to be about forty years old and spoke passable English. Fantini told the group that he was a former Peruvian Air Force pilot and had recently retired. He said that he was able to make a comfortable living in Iquitos flying tourists over the Amazon River so that they could see what the "Amazon jungle really looked like."

Dr. Machado asked Fantini if he knew anything about the Tageiri tribe of Waorani Indians and whether he had ever flown over that part of Peru where the Nashino and Cononaco Rivers joined. Fantini said no, and replied, "You are the only person who has ever asked me to fly into Tageiri territory." Fantini pointed out that the government of Peru had a Department of Indigenous Indian Affairs and that he had repeatedly heard that these Tageiri were dangerous and extremely hostile to outsiders. "Dr. Machado, I hope you know what you are getting into," said Fantini.

The *Bismarck* continued on downstream, and the sun began to set below the banks of the Amazon. Looking forward and to the port side, the great Napo River could be seen. The captain made a sweeping left turn, and the tug headed upstream on the Napo. The passengers could feel the tug losing headway as it now battled against the flow of the river. Darkness had fallen and the tug was alone on the Napo. Eventually, the lights of the small river outpost of Francisco de Orellana could be made out and the *Bismarck* dropped anchor. The biological station was nearby, and Dr. Machado had promised the next day would be spent visiting the famous canopy walkway.

On the next morning, Captain Krueger moved the *Bismarck* to the Explornado Camp, and Dr. Machado took Max and Anne ashore to visit the camp. Dr. Machado wanted to spend the day with the director so as to get as much information as possible with which to locate the Tageiris. He recommended that Anne and Max spend the day at the biological lab where the canopy was located. He also told them to be sure to see the giant Amazonian water lilies. It was agreed that they would regroup with the tug captain at sunset to make plans for the trip up the Napo.

The camp lay inland from the Napo River and consisted mainly of simple sleeping platforms for those tourists adventurous enough to go into the Amazon rain forest. A guide pointed to a trail that led to the canopy, and Max and Anne took off. The trail went through a thick primary forest teeming with insects and innumerable birds darting about. The trail was dark and water appeared to be dripping and seeping everywhere. Eventually they came to a small clearing above which could be seen a hanging canvas canopy that appeared to be about a hundred feet above ground. The canopy went through the very top of the rain forest and appeared to be about one half mile long. The rain forest growth was so thick that no sunlight reached the forest floor except in occasional clearings.

A guide appeared and showed the pair to a rope ladder, which allowed access to the suspended walkway. The guide explained that the canopy had been constructed by the biological lab because biologists had recently discovered a great number of birds and insect species, previously unknown, living in the canopy of the rain forest. The guide explained that these species existed entirely in the canopy amongst flora that had never been examined by tropical biologists. The guide wished them a pleasant visit and left.

Max and Anne spent the day poking about the canopy, marveling at the abundance of plant and animal life that made its home in the top of the rain forest. Countless small birds of every color and description darted about; monkeys yelled and screamed constantly; butterflies performed graceful aeronautical displays before their eyes and caterpillars and snakes crawled everywhere. Mosquitoes and gnats swirled about and the whole atmosphere felt heavy with every form of living thing. Frogs were everywhere. The place appeared to be a gigantic pulsating laboratory of tropical life. Anne wondered if it were possible that beneficial chemicals were being manufactured within this environment. Elated by their experience, they made their way back to the *Bismarck* as the sun began to set.

Night had fallen by the time the group had reassembled on the *Bismarck,* and Captain Krueger decided to remain at anchor for the night. Moreover, he had studied the charts of the Napo River provided by Dr. Machado and wanted to have a meeting to decide how to proceed during the next leg of the journey. He asked Max, Anne and Dr. Machado to join him in the wheelhouse after supper. The trio proceeded to the wheelhouse and found the captain bent over the maps at the tiny chartroom behind the wheel. He told them to pull up a stool and the group gathered about the maps of the region.

Captain Krueger spoke first. "Okay," he said, "we are on the Napo, which will eventually lead us into the Tageiri territory. The question is, which tributary river do we want to take after we get up the Napo in order to get close to that part of the jungle they are said to be inhabiting? What is your information on this point?"

Dr. Machado spoke. "Here is the latest information: I have spoken with Waorani shamen in Quito and Iquitos, the governmental authorities on Indian affairs in Iquitos, and the director of this lab. No one knows exactly where they live because they are constantly moving and avoid any contact with the white man. They also avoid the peaceful Waoranis, who live in the protectorates in Ecuador. The group I am looking for have never, to my knowledge, been contacted by the white man. This group is called the Tageiris. What I have been told is that this group is said to live in the area between the Nashino and Cononaco Rivers, close to the Peruvian border with Ecuador. All the sources of my information say that this uncontacted band of Indians is moving eastward, away from Ecuador, and toward Peru. They are said to be fleeing all contact with civilization."

Captain Krueger broke in. "That is a lot of jungle to explore. Do you have any landmark, any sort of guidepost we can search for?"

Dr. Machado was the only person who could answer this question. "The best information I have been able to obtain so far is that the Tageiri are living deep within the Amazon jungle, around a valley that contains their secret health garden. This garden is said to be somewhere between the Nashino and Cononaco rivers close to the border of Ecuador and Peru." Continuing, he said, "The Waorani shaman who gave me this information said that the entrance to this valley was from a grassy meadow above a large sandy bluff on the left side of a river, which was either a tributary of one of these rivers or a river that flowed into a tributary river. I was told that the sandy bluff would be on the left as one looked downstream and that it would be at a point on the river where it made a sharp curve to the north. The bluff is sandy and would be about fifty to a hundred feet above the river. At the top of the bluff and reaching to the edge of a dense jungle growth is a meadow about a thousand feet long, which stretched to the entrance of a long valley. This meadow is covered with a growth of grass but no trees. The shaman said that if one looked carefully, a faint path leading from the river to the valley containing the secret garden could be made out. He also told me that at the foot of this bluff is a curving sandy beach on which dugout canoes could be beached."

Poring over the map of the area just discussed, Captain Krueger said, "Very good; this gives us a destination point, at least." Pointing his finger along the Napo River on the map, he continued, "We will sail upstream to the junction of the Curaray River with the Napo, take the Curaray upstream to its junction with both the Cononaco and Nashino rivers. We can then go west on the Cononaco past the border of Ecuador and Peru and start our search by air. At this point we will be between the Nashino and Cononaco Rivers."

"Agreed," replied Dr. Machado and the group retired for the night.

Morning broke and the tug's crew began preparations to get underway. It was a beautiful day and the entire expedition party was excited. The anchor was raised and the tug headed toward the center of the Napo River. Max and Anne were seated on chairs just below the wheelhouse when Captain Krueger let out a yell, "Look to the port side. Those two fishermen are about to spear a Paiche."

Max and Anne looked toward the left bank of the Napo and saw a small dugout canoe with two Indians standing within it. The Indian closest to the bow had a long black spear fitted with a metal harpoon tip. The other was slowly sculling the dugout alongside a huge, primitive-looking fish, which was swimming slowly upstream on the surface. Captain Krueger guided the tug close to the scene and then shut down the engine. The dugout drew almost alongside the fish, which seemed totally unaware of its present danger. The Indian with the harpoon then threw it with all his strength and it landed with a thud about a foot behind the Paiche's head. The great fish thrashed about for several minutes and then began to swim with all its strength upstream. The fisherman then began to let out great lengths of the line that was attached to the end of the spear. The fish dragged the canoe upriver until it reached a small tributary stream, which it entered and went from view.

Captain Krueger spoke. "You have just seen how these Indians catch a fish that can weigh up to three hundred or more pounds. They let the Paiche swim about dragging their canoe until it is exhausted. Then they drag it ashore and cut off its head and tail and gut it. They cut the body of the fish into several pieces and then take it to port where it is sold."

Max and Anne had wondered how these Indians could possibly get this huge fish into their small dugout canoe, and now they knew. Both marveled at the fact that these Indians had used the whaling techniques of the Atlantic whalers to catch this largest fish of the Amazon. Captain Krueger restarted the engine and the last leg of the voyage into the Loreto and toward the land of the Tageiri got underway.

Everyone aboard soon settled down into an individual routine, and the days passed peacefully by as the tug headed in a general northwesterly direction up the river. Dr. Machado had advised the group that the tug was neither designed nor equipped for passengers, so it was understood that each group would do its own cooking. The captain and his assistant occupied the meager quarters; Dr. Machado's group slept in sleeping bags on the stern as did the helicopter pilot Fantini. The captain was gracious enough to allow everyone the use of the single toilet and the galley could be used for making coffee and warming up canned food.

Dr. Machado and Max had agreed that it would be wise to give the pilot Fantini the details of the trip. Max obtained the maps from the chartroom and showed Fantini the map that displayed the area where the Nashino and Cononaco joined. This was close to Bellavista, very near Peru's border with Ecuador. Fantini examined the area closely and said, "The area you want to fly over is fairly large, and we have only a general area where this sandy bluff is located. I recommend we get additional fuel further upstream, possibly at Copal Urco. And another thing. I hope you understand that this general area around Bellavista is very dangerous and I'm not talking about Indians."

"What do you mean?" replied Dr. Machado.

"This area is where some of the strongest and most expensive coca and marijuana crops are produced," continued Fantini. "There is a lot of gang activity in the area and the Peruvian government can't get it under control."

"Do you think these gangs would be about in the jungle where we are going?" asked Dr. Machado.

Fantini replied, "I don't know. I'm trying to tell you that you have selected the most dangerous area in the Loreto for your expedition."

The next several days were spent steaming toward Copal Urco. The *Bismarck* labored against the strong current of the Napo, and it appeared that it was moving northwesterly at about five knots. Everyone aboard had settled into a comfortable daily routine. Max and Anne took chairs up to the bow and spent the day watching the river scene. Dr. Machado chatted away with the pilot, Fantini, and Amö kept to himself. It was readily apparent that Amö was in his element. His face shone with the excitement and anticipation of exploring an area once the domain of his ancestors. Amö took pleasure in spotting the varied fauna of the region, happily pointing out the monkeys and sloths that seem to be everywhere in the trees growing at the very edge of the river's banks. It was almost as if Amö had designated himself the group's tour guide. White egrets and multi-colored macaws flew about, and pink dolphins surfaced about the tug. It seemed hard to believe that the group was entering into dangerous territory.

Max and Anne noticed that the native Indians seemed to fish very close to shore. They appeared to concentrate on shallow pools near the banks of the Napo. They also noticed that small villages appeared every few miles, always built very near the river banks. No roads leading into the jungle could be seen. No Indians were ever seen walking in the jungle. The Napo and the innumerable small rivers that flowed into each bank of the Napo were the roads of the Amazon jungle. Both Max and Anne commented that the jungle growth on each bank extended to the very edge of the river. They wondered how any human could possibly get far into the interior of the jungle.

Captain Krueger had decided that he would anchor his vessel each night because he had never navigated the Napo and there were no buoys marking the deeper part of the river. Above all, he feared going hard aground on some hidden sand bar in the river.

Eventually, the *Bismarck* reached Copal Urco and additional fuel was taken aboard as the group spent a few hours ashore. The tug cast off again and steamed westerly to the junction of the Napo with the Curaray River. The expedition would then enter the Curaray River and steam upstream to where the Cononaco River flowed into it, very near the border between Peru and Ecuador. It was at this point where a decision had to be made as to when and where the search by helicopter was to begin.

In the early afternoon of the next day, the *Bismarck* entered the Curaray River and began the final northwesterly leg of the journey. The Curaray was a smaller river than the Napo, and the water seemed to be a bit cleaner and less riddled with debris than either the Napo or the Amazon.

Max and Anne had, on several occasions, wondered how the indigenous people could possibly have survived drinking the waters of the Amazon. These waters were either a dark, dirty brown or a black color containing quantities of floating logs and branches from the jungle. Dead fish and birds could be seen everywhere floating on the surface of the river. The waters were heavy with the sediments of the jungle floor and, at each village, one saw buckets lined up near the river bank, which the natives used to filter out the mud and dirt from the river water. Amö had spoken of the health problem these people had to endure from all sorts of parasitic intestinal infections.

After steaming upstream for several days, every vestige of human civilization disappeared. No villages, no Indians fishing in dugouts could be seen. The *Bismarck* seemed to be in the middle of a great, dense jungle, alone on a small tributary of the Napo.

As the tug steamed closer to the border of Ecuador, a subtle but pervasive change took place in the mood aboard the vessel. A faint, but perceptible, sense of foreboding began to assert itself. Idle conversation seemed to have ended and everyone aboard took on a pensive look. Dr. Machado wondered aloud if the Tageiris had chased off the Waorani population. Amö was asked his opinion. All he could offer was that "this country used to be the territory of my ancestors."

The *Bismarck* moved closer to the border of Ecuador, and Captain Krueger decided upon extra precaution. He pointed out that the river was narrowing as they steamed northwest, which would make it easier for a dugout to draw alongside his tug. He recommended an armed watch during the night when the *Bismarck* was at anchor. Everyone agreed and it was decided that each man would share the night watch with an alarm bell nearby. Dr. Machado had brought a shotgun and two rifles aboard so the vessel was well-armed.

Several days passed as the tug beat northwest up the river. No Indians could be seen. It seemed as if only the tug and its occupants were about in this part of the jungle. At last, the *Bismarck* reached the confluence of the Cononaco, the Nashino, and the Curary rivers. The tug dropped anchor where the three rivers joined and the expedition settled in for the night. The captain decided that in the morning he would call a meeting to decide the further course the tug would take.

The next morning Captain Krueger asked Max, Dr. Machado, and Amö to join him in the wheelhouse. The group gathered about a large map spread on the chartroom table. Pointing with the tip of his dividers, the captain said, "Here is where we are on the Curary. We can either continue west on the Cononaco or we can go north on the Nashino. What do you think, Doctor?"

Dr. Machado replied, "I think we are close to Tageiri territory. I have been told that they are in a valley between the Nashino and Cononaco rivers and are near the Peruvian border. It is also rumored that they might be near the Shiripuno River, which flows into the Cononaco west of here. Let me ask Amö." An extended conversation between Amö and Dr. Machado ensued, using Spanish, Quichua and some Waorani. Dr. Machado continued, "Amö makes a good point. He says that the Nashino River flows through an Ecuadorian national park, which is located at the border of Ecuador and Peru. He believes these 'Aucas,' as he calls the Tageiris, would never settle at or near a park visited by the white man. Amö suggests that we go west on the Cononaco and anchor the tug at that point on the map where the two rivers are nearest to each other. I agree."

"Done," said the captain. "We will steam west for a couple of days on the Cononaco and drop anchor. We will also be close enough to the Shiripuno if we want to fly over it." The *Bismarck* raised anchor, and the expedition continued toward the land of the Tageiri.

Two days later the *Bismarck* dropped anchor at that point on the Cononaco River that flowed closest to the Nashino. Preparations began to explore the area by helicopter. Dr. Machado had arranged for a radio communication setup so that there could be constant contact between the helicopter and the *Bismarck* and also, constant communication between any group in the jungle and the *Bismarck*.

A general aerial search plan was agreed upon. Captain Krueger and the deck hand would remain aboard the tug with Anne. Fantini would fly the helicopter with Max, Dr. Machado, and Amö as passengers. The first aerial sweep of the expedition would commence in the early afternoon.

Fantini had told Max and Dr. Machado that he had flown many aerial reconnaissance missions as a Peruvian air force pilot. Fantini examined the maps of the river and was told about the sandy bluff that marked the entrance to the secret valley of the Tageiri. He remarked that the Nashino appeared to be only about fifty or seventy-five miles north of the Cononaco and that both rivers flowed in a generally easterly direction in the area. He told the group that his helicopter had an approximate range of 250 miles and could stay aloft around three hours or so. It was agreed that they would fly north until they reached the Nashino and then take sweeps to the left and right to see if the bluff could be located. The cables securing the helicopter to the wooden deck were freed and the craft took off. Fantini told his passengers that he would fly directly north until he reached the Nashino River and then turn east and fly in the middle of the corridor created by the two rivers. He would fly in this direction for about forty-five minutes and if nothing was found would turn around to go west for about ninety minutes. Fantini concluded by saying that if nothing was seen, he would then return to the *Bismarck* and try another direction tomorrow.

The helicopter rapidly gained attitude and headed due north toward the Nashino River. Fantini leveled off at about five hundred feet above the canopy of the jungle, giving the passengers an excellent opportunity to search the ground below. Everywhere one looked, the vista was the same: an endless basin of thick, green jungle. No human habitation was seen; no Indian appeared anywhere. Max stared out of the left side of the craft while Amö looked to the right. Startled birds flew about in great clusters and numerous animals were spotted darting about on the jungle floor. Great Ceiba trees were growing everywhere and strangler fig vines appeared as natural ropes leading from the canopy to the floor of the forest. Max wondered how anyone, even a native Indian, could move through this maze of jungle growth.

The helicopter reached the Nashino and Fantini turned right to fly east toward the Ecuadorian border. He then began a series of S-like sweeps across the jungle area that lay between the two rivers. Max noted numerous rivers, not shown on the river maps supplied by the Peruvian government, which ran into both the Cononaco and Nashino rivers. All the rivers seemed to flow toward the east. It seemed clear that there was a natural tilt in the floor of the Amazon basin toward the Atlantic Ocean. No sign of the sandy bluff appeared; Fantini made a U-turn and flew west, repeating the same curving, snakelike flight as the copter headed west. He reached the westerly end of his search along the corridor, and, again, nothing was found. The helicopter headed back to the *Bismarck* as the sun began to set. It was nearly dark as the craft settled down onto its landing platform.

On the following day, the group reviewed again the maps of the major rivers in the area and decided to spend the entire day flying east, toward Bellavista in Peru and then returning west, above that portion of the jungle near the Cononaco River. The helicopter spent almost six hours in the air, and no river bank fitting the description given to Dr. Machado by the shaman appeared.

On the next morning, Dr. Machado decided to seek Amö's recommendation. Max took all the river maps out of the wheelhouse and placed them on the deck of the *Bismarck* so that everyone present could have a good look at the area. Amö began to carefully examine the topography of that map covering the area where the Shiripuno River ran southerly into the Cononaco. He said, "This is wild and primitive country. This is land where the Waorani might live and where the 'Aucas' might be found." Upon hearing this, Max asked Captain Krueger to move the *Bismarck* west to where the Shiripuno flowed into the Cononaco. The westerly steam up the Cononaco took the remainder of the day, and as twilight approached, the expedition dropped anchor at the junction of the two rivers.

117

It was immediately clear that the expedition had reached the most inaccessible and inhospitable part of the Amazon basin river system. There was absolutely no sign of human life; there was no evidence that any human civilization had reached this part of the jungle. The group settled in for the night. It was agreed that, in the morning, the next aerial search would begin.

It was noted that, at the point on the map where the *Bismarck* was at anchor, both the Cononaco and Shiripuno rivers flowed in a general southeasterly direction. On the following morning, it was decided to explore the westerly portions of the Shiripuno, which flowed east about thirty-five miles to the north of the Cononaco. The morning flight revealed no sign of the sandy bluff the party was searching for. The only thing seen was endless miles of thick jungle through which the Cononaco River flowed. The river seemed to be fed by countless tributary systems, but no topography matching that for which they searched came into view. The helicopter returned to the *Bismarck*, refueled, and the group prepared for the afternoon flight.

In the afternoon the search party took off. Fantini decided to fly north following the course of the Shiripuno. After a flight of about forty miles, the river divided. One branch went toward the west; the other branch went north for about fifty miles and then flowed in a general southeasterly direction.

At Max's request, the helicopter turned left and flew along to the branch of the river that flowed from west to east. Finding nothing, the helicopter flew north, and picked up what appeared to be a tributary river of the Shiripuno, and followed it as the river flowed east. As the helicopter flew over a rise in the basin, it could be seen that the tributary river was taking a sharp turn toward the north. Suddenly Max yelled, "Look, Roberto, there it is!" Directly below them and to the left was a sandy bluff above a sandy beach where the river curved toward the north. They had found the place that the shaman had described as the entrance to the valley of the Tageiri.

Fantini decided to circle his helicopter directly over the meadow above the beach. It was covered with thick grass and scattered bushes but no trees. It appeared to stretch north for about a thousand feet where it ended at the edge of the jungle. It was a perfect place to land the helicopter. Fantini radioed Captain Krueger that the bluff had been located and flew back to the tug.

That evening proved to be the most festive night for the expedition since the last evening in Iquitos at the Bombeleo. Captain Krueger brought out some beer and wine for the joyous group, which sensed that the trip was to end in success. Bruening brought out his accordion and played a variety of German and American songs. Tomorrow they would surely find the secret garden of the Tageiris.

The next morning was spent on preparations for the search for the valley. It was agreed that the *Bismarck* would be moved to a point about ten miles downstream of the sandy bluff where it would remain at anchor while the land search was carried out. This might avoid the possibility of being discovered by the Tageiris. The helicopter would then fly the search group onto the meadow and then return to the tug. The search group would be equipped with a radio so as to be able to be in constant contact with the tug. Dr. Machado would carry a shotgun and a pistol; Max would be armed with a rifle and pistol. Amö would carry a machete and the necessary camping equipment.

By early afternoon the *Bismarck* had anchored near the sandy bluff and the helicopter flew the group to the meadow and then headed back to the tug. Dr. Machado, Max, Anne and Amö found themselves alone on a vast meadow that stretched north to the edge of the forest. Amö examined the ground carefully, but no clear footpath could be seen.

The meadow was covered with thick, strong grass and occasional clumps of bushes. Faint footprints could be made out, but it was evident that this was not an area frequented by many people. The jungle forest lay to the north so the group started north to see if some kind of entrance to the forest could be found.

Upon reaching the end of the meadow, they saw that the ground began to slope downward toward the west and seemed to provide a natural path to the valley that could be seen far below. There was a large rise on either side of the path where large bushes and trees grew. They followed the path until it ended at the great forest, which guarded the entrance into the valley. From this point onward, they would have to find their way through the jungle.

Upon reaching the jungle growth, it was decided that Amö would lead the group, followed by Dr. Machado, then Anne, with Max bringing up the rear. Upon entering the forest, it could be seen that this would be the most difficult part of their search. Easy movement was impossible. The jungle was a thick mass of vines, bushes, trees, and vegetation. No clear path could be seen, so Amö took that path that appeared to head downward toward the bottom of the valley they were entering. Amö cautioned the group to be very careful to examine every branch or vine in the forest before grabbing hold in order to avoid poisonous snakes.

The jungle was alive with masses of mosquitoes and other insects, creating a living hell as the group passed on. The floor of the jungle also presented a danger as the group had to pass over or through areas covered with mud and water.

On several occasions the path chosen by Amö would lead nowhere and the group would have to turn back and start down another path. Amö decided to mark each mile of the paths taken by cutting down strangler fig vines on each side of the path so that the return trip would be made easier. The forest growth seemed to become more dense as each mile was traveled and the light grew ever darker. The going became so difficult that it took nearly two hours to cover one mile. Eventually, it became apparent that night was approaching, and the party made preparations to spend their first night alone in the Amazon jungle. A small clearing was located and the tent set up. Amö thought that it would be too dangerous to start a campfire, so the night was spent in total darkness. The men agreed to stand a constant rotating night watch as the group attempted to get some sleep throughout a night filled with strange and frightening sounds.

All night long Anne lay curled in a fetal position in her sleeping bag, expecting that, at any minute, disaster would strike. It seemed as if the night would never end. Max began to wonder if all the effort and expense was worth enduring this ordeal.

At long last, the morning came and the group began to resume the trek through the jungle. Just as they were about to start out, Amö said to Dr. Machado, "I had a dream last night; I saw the Aucas. They were staring at me with eyes full of hate. They called me 'outsider.' I am afraid, Doctor. I will return to the meadow and wait there for you. Always take the path that will lead downward to the valley floor. Mark your path as I did yesterday." Amö handed his machete to Dr. Machado and without saying another word turned and walked away.

Everyone was stunned, but Dr. Machado seemed determined to make the best of it. "I will lead; Max, you bring up the rear; Anne, you stay in the middle," he said. Before starting out, Dr. Machado took a good look about. "Look," he exclaimed, "that might be the valley floor." He pointed to a clearing in the jungle, about five or six miles below, through which a small river flowed. "With luck, we could make it by nightfall."

The day dragged on as the trio made its way toward the valley floor. On many occasions the path chosen became so narrow that it became necessary to walk sideways. Sometimes the path would have to be cleared of dense growths of vines and tree branches. Slowly and painfully they inched forward. As the afternoon drew to a close, it became apparent that the jungle was thinning and that the floor of the valley was near. As darkness approached, they broke through the last barrier of the forest and saw, less than one hundred yards away, the open expanse of the valley floor. They decided to camp for the night and to explore the secret garden in the morning.

The morning found the group in a more optimistic mood. After a Spartan breakfast, they took a look around and found that the topography of the valley floor matched in every detail the description given to Dr. Machado by the Waorani shaman.

The valley floor appeared to be several miles long and about two hundred yards wide. Through the valley a small stream flowed and on each side of the stream grew trees that had never been seen when they worked their way through the jungle. They noticed that the dense jungle through which they had just passed stopped abruptly about a hundred yards from the valley floor. It seemed as if some unknown force had decreed a separation had to exist between the edge of the jungle and the edge of the jungle floor. The river appeared to flow from west to east, and on each side of the river could be seen thick growths of cruciferous plants. At that point where the plant growth ended, the strange new trees could be found.

Dr. Machado grew increasingly agitated as he began his inspection of the secret garden. He asked Anne and Max to join him as he walked through the cruficerae that lined the banks of the small river. On the north side of the river, the plants appeared to be a giant species of brussel sprouts. He dropped to the ground, broke off a single sprout, and handed it to Anne. The sprout was absolutely huge; a green mass larger than a golf ball, emitting an unmistakably medicinal odor. He then dug out a large portion of the root structure of the plant and pointed out how strong and sinewy the root appeared. He opened an extra backpack he had brought along and placed several examples of the sprout and root structure of the plant into the pack.

Dr. Machado pointed to the ground upon which the plant grew. "Look," he said, "there isn't a weed of any kind growing about these plants. Look at the leaves. There is no evidence of any damage whatsoever by any insect or caterpillar or other bug. This plant is obviously manufacturing a strong repellant chemical of some type." Pointing out a large portion of the ground with a wave of his arm, Dr. Machado continued, "Do you see a single ant about?" he asked. "The Amazon is home to the greatest collection of ants in the world, yet none are here. We must find out why."

Dr. Machado asked Max and Anne to follow him to the south side of the river. Here was found another species of cruciferous plant, which appeared to be giant cauliflower. The white portion of the plant growth seemed to be the size of a basketball and, again, it was seen that the plant appeared to be completely free of any type of damage. It also gave off a strong chemical smell. Dr. Machado gathered up several large specimens of the plant and stored them in his pack.

They spent the remainder of the morning inspecting the floor of the valley. They could find no evidence of insect damage anywhere; they could find no evidence of damage by birds or by the fauna of the jungle. The valley floor seemed protected by some form of antiseptic manufactured by the flora found in the vicinity.

The afternoon was given to an examination of the trees that grew about the valley floor. On the north side of the river grew a tree that appeared to be a variety of the mahogany species. Its trunk appeared to be incredibly strong, resembling a palm tree. The trunk was covered by a thin layer of black bark. It appeared to grow to a height of about one hundred feet. Dr. Machado cut off several large portions of bark and also a portion of the root structure of the tree and placed the specimens in his pack. He noted that the tree trunks of these mahogany-type trees bore no evidence of damage or intrusion whatsoever.

Crossing again to the south bank of the river, he examined the trees on that side. They appeared to be similar to the ceiba tree, except in color and thickness of bark. The tree was dark brown in color with a root structure that created a buttress formation on the ground. The bark of this tree was much thinner than the bark of the jungle ceiba. There were no strangler fig vines dangling from the branches of these trees and absolutely no evidence of any insect damage could be found. Both of these species of trees seemed to have created a perfect immunity system, protecting it from its natural enemies. Dr. Machado gathered his specimens from this ceiba-like tree and stored them away. Evening approached and the party made preparations to spent the night in the garden of the Tageiris.

As dawn came to the valley floor, Dr. Machado was already up and about. He had spent a restless and mostly sleepless night reviewing the conclusions he had drawn upon inspecting the valley floor that day. His mind was full of both contradictions and feelings of elation. On the one hand, he was certain that he had found the secret health garden described by the Waorani shaman in Iquitos. He had noticed that, in walking about the entire length and width of the valley floor, he had seen no evidence of mosquitoes, ticks, gnats, or any other insect that infest the Amazon basin. He had noted that no birds of any kind were flying either in or above the garden. He had observed that the jungle growth through which they had so laboriously traveled ended well short of that point at which the cruciferae grew. He had pointed out to Max and Anne that both the trees and the plant growth showed no evidence of damage from attacks by insects, birds, or other natural enemies. It seemed obvious that some chemical or medicinal agent was at work, which, in effect, was immunizing or sanitizing the area. Dr. Machado had concluded that these conditions were not the results of chance. Could this be the medicine for which they searched?

On the other hand, Dr. Machado began to be overwhelmed by a nagging sense of foreboding. Like Amö, he began to suspect that his group was being spied upon. He felt it imperative to leave the valley at once. They had intruded enough into the land of the Tageiri. Nudging the sleeping forms of Max and Anne awake, he said, "It is time to get going. Let's leave in thirty minutes." The camping equipment was repacked for travel, and after a bit of breakfast, the trio began to retrace their steps to return to the meadow.

Dr. Machado knew that the return trip would be far easier than their descent into the valley. The path was now clearly marked, and there would be no time lost because of wrongful detours, which had caused so many delays during entry. Dr. Machado radioed Fantini and said that he would be getting a call to return to the meadow around three or four that afternoon. With Dr. Machado leading the way, they headed up valley toward the meadow.

The hike uphill from the valley floor, though arduous, went uneventfully; Max and Dr. Machado divided the heavy packs while Anne carried the firearms. The morning went by as the group trudged upward. About noon they reached the area of the path at which they had camped on the first night into the jungle. They rested for about a half hour, drank some water, and continued on toward the meadow. An hour went by. Suddenly Dr. Machado let out a horrified yell. Pointing up the marked path, he said, "My god! It's Amö!" Not one hundred feet ahead the body of Amö lay, face up, across the jungle path. Three black chonta wood spears, each about ten feet long, had entered his body. Two spears had passed through his chest; one had gone through his abdomen. It was apparent that the spears had anchored Amö's body firmly to the path. On the upper end of each spear dangled a circular balsa wood ear plug, its lower portion covered with a bright white paint. The plugs appeared to be attached to the spear with brown fibers woven together into a thin string. Dr. Machado's premonition had come true. They had been observed; they were being watched. He said, "The Tageiris are near us. Those earplugs with white paint mean 'Outsider, get out!' "

Near panic began to overcome the group. Anne began to scream and fell to the ground, crying and yelling for what seemed to be an eternity of time. Max did what he could to console her; it was obvious that there was nothing that could be said to diminish the horror of the scene that they had come upon.

Dr. Machado attempted to get the situation under control. He ran up to where Amö lay and examined the body. "His body is cold and stiff. He has been dead for many hours, perhaps for a day," said Dr. Machado. "We must get out of here and onto the meadow as quickly as possible."

Dr. Machado instantly decided to abandon all the heavy camping gear, and the group started uphill again, carrying only their backpacks and firearms. Not a word was spoken as they alternated in running and walking up the marked path. Three hours of forced march went by in conditions of utter terror. Anne's face had gone white with fear; Dr. Machado and Max looked grim, and each clutched his weapon close to his chest. Nearing exhaustion, they reached a clearing through which the edge of the forest could be seen. Just beyond lay the rise of a small hill, which bordered the edge of the meadow. Dr. Machado calculated that within twenty minutes they would pass over the hill and would enter upon the north edge of the meadow. He radioed Fantini to land the helicopter as close as possible to the north edge of the meadow.

Within moments they had cleared the jungle and were walking up the path, which sloped downward toward the west. This was the path they had taken to enter the forest. Reaching the crest of the hill, they only had to pass through the part of the sloping path, which was bordered on both sides by trees and large thick bushes. Directly ahead and to their right, the expanse of the meadow could be clearly seen. At any moment the helicopter would land and their terrible ordeal would end.

They passed over the hill and through the path bordered by the trees and large bushes and turned south to reach the meadow. They had traveled not more than two hundred yards when Max said, "Bruno, look behind you!" Standing on the rise of the hill they had just passed and between the bushes and the trees was a group of perhaps forty Indian warriors. They appeared to have materialized out of nowhere. Retreat back into the jungle was now impossible.

Temporarily paralyzed by fear, the trio did nothing. They saw that the group of Indians had begun to form a semicircle, walking in a sort of lock-step toward them. As the Indians moved closer, it could be seen that each warrior was carrying both a spear and a blowgun in his right hand. Each warrior had a round balsa wood plug in each earlobe and slashes of white paint on each cheek. In the center of the group stood a taller warrior, wearing a headdress of white feathers. His voice trembling, Dr. Machado said, "These are the Tageiri."

The Indians continued to move slowly toward Dr. Machado's group, then suddenly stopped. They began to speak in an agitated manner, pointing toward the river with their spears. The trio looked to the south and saw that Fantini's helicopter was approaching. Soon the beating sounds of the rotors could be heard and, with a great swoop, the craft landed about one hundred yards away. The Indians began to jump up and down and to gesticulate wildly. It was obvious that they had never seen a helicopter before and were astonished that such a contraption existed.

In a few moments, the Tageiris quieted down and each group stared at the other. It appeared that each group didn't know what next to do. Dr. Machado radioed Fantini to keep the helicopter running, pointing toward the band of Indians to the north.

The reluctant truce ended when the Tageiri chief shouted, "Kowudi! (outsider). What Kowudi want in land of Tageiri? You want oil?"

"No," replied Dr. Machado. "We have white shaman with us. We look for Tageiri medicine to cure cancer."

"What cancer?" replied the chief.

"Cancer sickness that kills from inside out," said Dr. Machado. "No fever, no pain until end. Body shrivels, heart stops, white man dies."

The chief continued, "Tageiri no have this disease. Tageiri always strong until meet Kowudi."

A few moments of silence ensued. Dr. Machado couldn't decide what to do. Conversation seemed both difficult and pointless. He did not want to make a run for the helicopter, feeling certain that these young warriors could easily overtake his group.

The chief broke the impasse. "Warrior say you take tree bark and plants from Tageiri health garden. This valley sacred to Tageiri. Put on meadow or we kill!" Without a word, Dr. Machado opened the backpack containing the specimens and, with exaggerated gestures, spilled its contents upon the ground. "Kowudi men, go to iron bird," said the chief. "Woman, stay on the meadow. Chief want white woman!"

Dr. Machado sensed that a crisis was approaching, "No," he replied. "Woman belongs to me." With that the chief shouted out some commands to his warriors. The group became agitated and started to shuffle about.

A drum began to beat and the chief's face took a bestial and violent look. He cried out, "Chief want to see ass of white woman!"

"Drop your pants, Anne," ordered Dr. Machado. "Maybe this will calm him down." Anne looked at the chief and saw that he was working himself into a savage rage. All the muscles of his upper body began to tighten; his face began to assume an apelike appearance. Turning away from the chief, she unzipped her pants, which fell to the ground. Her beautiful rear now faced the leering mob. The savage band went crazy. The drum was being pounded at fever pitch; the chief began to wave a machete in the air. He yelled, "Chief take woman to long house!"

Dr. Machado knew an attack was imminent. Grabbing his radio, he said, "Roberto, I think they are going to kill

Max and me and take Anne; take the helicopter aloft and fly over them as closely as you can. This might frighten them. Then come back and land near us. We can make a run for it."

With a great roar from the rotors and amidst gusting winds, the helicopter went upward. Putting on full power, Fantini flew directly at the band of Indians. They became terrified and, abandoning their weapons, threw themselves upon the ground. The roar from the threshing rotor blades was deafening. With a graceful swoop, the helicopter made a complete turn and landed near Dr. Machado. Fantini threw open the cabin door.

Dr. Machado saw that a chance to escape had come. "Anne, make a dash for it; we will cover you." Anne gathered herself together and, running with all her strength, made it to the door. Max and Dr. Machado unlocked the safety catch on their weapons and began to walk backward toward the helicopter door. The helicopter maneuver had seemed, at least temporarily, to have disorganized the Tageiris. Step by step they inched closer to safety.

Just as the end to the drama seemed near, a young and powerful Tageiri broke from the group and began to run at full speed toward Max and Dr. Machado. He moved toward the pair with incredible grace and speed, his spear raised in readiness. Dr. Machado knew that the moment had come for desperate action. He had sensed that they could never get to the door before the Tageiri got within killing range. "Max, take a shot at him; aim for his chest. If you miss, I will get him when he gets within range of my shotgun." Max dropped to one knee and took aim with his rifle as the warrior ran toward him. A shot rang out and, almost instantly, a great splotch of blood appeared on the Tageiri's chest. The Tageiri fell to the ground. A few of the nearest warriors ran up to their kin and stared in disbelief at his dead body. They had never seen the blowgun of the Kowudi in action.

This momentary delay had given Max and the doctor their chance. They sprinted to the helicopter and climbed aboard. By this time the chief had ordered his warriors to charge, but the helicopter flew clear before the Tageiris could get close enough to release their spears.

As Fantini flew his exhausted passengers back to the tug, Dr. Machado radioed Captain Krueger to raise anchor. The helicopter soon landed and the *Bismarck* made a complete turn and headed downstream toward Iquitos. Upon reaching port, the expedition disbanded and Max made preparations to fly with Anne to New York.

XII

The Thirteenth Disciple

Their Amazon adventure having failed, Max and Anne flew home to New York after a final dinner with Dr. Machado in San Jose. Dr. Machado had suggested that it might be possible to obtain protection by the military if another expedition into Waorani territory were to be planned, but for now, Anne's dream had ended and both wanted to return to New York and regroup.

Max was in great spirits and insisted upon checking into a suite at the Waldorf Astoria Hotel. Max had fallen madly in love with Anne and wanted to figure out a plan whereby their relationship could continue. Perhaps they could go to Central America and examine the area around Teotichuacan or perhaps Anne would agree to a trip to China. Max was agreeable to anything so long as they stayed together. Anne wanted to get to the agency and see what was going on and, above all, to tell her friends about her glorious adventure. They spent a quiet evening about the hotel, glad to be back in civilization again.

The next morning they had a leisurely breakfast in the hotel. Anne had called the Middlethorpe Agency and had been advised to be there at 3:00 P.M. for a "most important meeting." Middy had not gone into details other than to tell Anne that the biggest deal in her career would be discussed.

Anne wanted to visit with her model friends around New York before the meeting, so she planned to spend the entire day in the city. Max had called Amy in California to let her know what happened in the Amazon and also to tell Amy that he was going to ask Anne to be his constant companion. Max told his daughter that he was going to make Anne an offer that he hoped she "couldn't refuse." It was decided as breakfast ended that they would meet at 7:00 P.M. in the Waldorf dining room where they could dine and discuss the day's activities. Anne left to start her day, and Max decided to spend a leisurely day walking around Manhattan and Central Park.

Max was in heaven; he felt strong, young, and completely recovered. All he could think about was Anne. He put on a tennis outfit and decided that he would walk to Central Park, take a long and peaceful stroll, and then find a nice tree to lie under as he worked out his "offer" to Anne. It was a beautiful, sunny day, and Max marveled as to how his life had changed in the past few months. He found it impossible to believe that a few months ago he had tried to kill himself.

Max worked his way up to Central Park, scarcely noticing the throngs of people rushing to and fro on the city streets. In his mind, his future was clear. He was going to live the rest of his life at full throttle with Anne and would give no further thought whatsoever to his cancer. He had earlier decided that he would make Anne "a proposition" at dinner, and if she agreed to it, they would plan out their next adventure. Max felt that his chances were reasonably good. He had more than enough money to do anything or go any place with Anne, and Anne seemed to be at a stage in her life where she wanted to get away from her career for a while.

For several hours Max walked around the park, totally absorbed in his thoughts. It was a working day for most people, and Max had the park almost to himself. He thought over every aspect of his proposed offer to Anne and ultimately found a shady spot in a secluded part of the park where he lay down to decide upon the final terms. He found himself thinking amidst a wonderfully peaceful garden scene.

Max did not want to go through a formal marriage. Though ever hopeful, he was realistic about his medical condition and doubted that his remission would be a permanent thing. He did not want to stand in her way if Anne should want out of the relationship and, above all, he didn't want to mess with lawyers and divorce court if it didn't work out. Max thought, *If these are the final years, why not make them the happiest and most peaceful of my life? I will make a generous provision for Amy and leave the rest of my estate to Anne provided she agrees to live with me until I die.*

Max had decided. That evening he would tell Anne that he would leave three-quarters of his entire estate to her if she would live with him until he died. He would tell Anne that he would go anywhere she wanted and do anything she wanted as long as they remained a team. It would be completely understood that Anne would leave him any time she desired. Max would prepare a new will that carried out their agreement and Anne would never have to work as long as he lived unless she so desired. They could continue to search for a cancer cure or move to the Riviera. Max was agreeable to anything. His heart bursting with happiness, Max made his way back to the hotel.

Seven o'clock arrived, and Anne walked into the Waldorf Astoria main dining room as Max awaited. The maitre d' gave one look at Miss Arpels and promptly assigned the couple to a "power table" where her youth and beauty could be appreciated by the guests pouring in for the evening. As soon as they were seated, Max sensed that trouble lay ahead. Anne seemed unduly animated; her face was flushed and her eyes flashed as though she could hardly wait to speak. A waiter arrived, cocktails were ordered and the menu read as Max waited with a sense of foreboding for Anne to start the conversation. "Max," she began, "we have got to talk." Max had heard that ominous phrase before and shuddered.

"Please," Max replied, "go ahead. I have all the time in the world."

Anne took a sip of her cocktail and focused her beautiful eyes upon Max. She looked resolute but a little sad, and Max prepared for the worst. "Today," she began, "I have been offered the greatest career opportunity of my life. I met an Italian man named Luca Stromboli who is a big movie producer in Florence. He has seen a number of my modeling skits at the agency and has offered me the lead in a picture to be made in Italy about the life of Christ. I am to play the part of Mary who will be eventually named 'Mary, a redeemer.' Max, the plot of this picture is fantastic and Stromboli thinks it could make me a star."

"Tell me about the plot," interjected Max, who was feeling worse by the minute.

Anne continued, "The plot calls for me to have a chance encounter with Jesus in Jerusalem. He has entered the city on his ass and chances upon me as I perform my dances in a public square. I play the part of a temptress; I sing, dance in a seductive way, and flaunt my figure in a suggestive manner. I am a sort of courtesan or geisha, although I do not do anything immoral. Call me a shill, if you will. I ply my trade for the coins thrown on the square by the amorous young men of Bethlehem. I make my living by utilizing my physical attributes.

"When my last dance has finished and as I gather up the money thrown upon the square by the cheering men, Jesus approaches and we begin to talk. He tells me of his ministry and what he hopes to accomplish by his preaching in the city. He gently admonishes me for using my physical beauty to appeal to the baser instincts of men and suggests that my physical gifts could be put to a higher use. He asks me to become his assistant and to travel everywhere with him in his ministry. I will be taught the ancient truths and the new gospel, and my function will be to assist him in converting young women to his new faith. Ours will be a true friendship based upon the love of God. I agree and we travel everywhere in Jerusalem on his ass. I sing and dance in a spiritual way, collect donations, and speak with and comfort the young women of Jerusalem who have gone astray. We re-enact many of the parables including that of the fallen woman, the making of wine at the wedding, and others. Gradually I realize how great a teacher Jesus is and decided to spend the rest of my life in his ministry. My whole life has changed and I have become a practicing Christian. My task is to assist Jesus in dealing with the problems of young women on the streets of this cruel city.

"The movie moves along in this manner, and we come to the evening of what is now universally called 'the Last Supper.' I am invited by Jesus to attend a dinner with the twelve disciples. At this dinner Jesus announced to the astonished group that I am to be the thirteenth disciple and that henceforth my name will be Mary, a Redeemer. At the table where Judas sits, audible sounds of discord can be heard and Judas says that 'it is written that the holy are to be men.' Despite opposition, Jesus insists and the last meal of Christ is concluded. The film ends at the Cross. As I plead to the Roman soldiers to stop, Christ is nailed to the cross as the soldiers beat upon me with their whips. I huddle at the foot of the cross as the blood of Jesus drips upon my shoulders. I dedicate the rest of my life to the spread of his gospel."

Max joined in. "It is a beautiful story. Tell me, what is the name of the picture?"

136

"An Ass for All Seasons," replied Anne. Both Anne and Max were silent for a few moments as each poked at the meal.

Conversations became difficult as Max instantly realized this could cause their first separation. "How long will it take to make the picture?" asked Max.

"About a year," replied Anne.

Max carried on, inwardly enraged that this Italian fellow had disrupted his plans. "What do you know about the character or morals of Stromboli? Where will you live? How do you know that Stromboli is adequately financed or that he will provide financial support for you during this year in Italy? Have you been given a financial statement? Are you able to interview any actors or actresses who have worked for Stromboli? Have you considered the possibility that you might be stranded in Florence without a dime to your name?" Max was jealous, inwardly conceding that he was lashing out at Anne.

Anne replied, "I don't have all of the details and only know that Stromboli is to be advised tomorrow whether his financial package has been approved by his bankers in Florence. Middy told me that he was very well recommended by an Italian client. He seems to be a perfect gentleman." Anne was becoming more and more defensive and showed it. "Max," she concluded, "this is the opportunity of a lifetime for me. I have always wanted to know whether I have the talent to make a movie. I may never get this chance again."

Max remained silent for a few moments and went over his options. He could make his pitch now or wait a year, hoping that Anne would get this movie business out of her system. He could appeal to her mercy, arguing that in a year he might be dead. But Max had come to know Anne well. He was certain that once Anne had chosen a course of action, she would carry it out. Concluding that further argument would be useless, Max wished her well.

A few silent moments passed. Then, Max said, "Tell me, did Stromboli ask you to dinner when the meeting was over?"

"Yes, he did," shot back Anne, obviously annoyed. "You know," said Anne. "You are acting like a jealous high school kid."

"Well," replied Max, "how do you know that this guy isn't trying to get you in bed?"

"Shut up, Max," replied Anne. "Do you think I'm some silly bimbo?" Anne's face flushed and she glared at Max. They had had their first fight.

A portentous gloom settled upon the table. It was most obvious that the meal was over. After what seemed an eternity, Anne told Max that she had made arrangements to stay the night with a girlfriend. Anne knew that Max would be upset that their relationship was ending. She did not want to spend the rest of the night arguing and, recognizing that Max was crushed, said goodnight. She promised to call Max in a few days when she had received the final details from Stromboli. Max sat for a few moments in dreary silence, paid the bill, and went to his suite. This was the first time during his entire relationship with Anne that he felt let down, tired and old.

Upon entering his suite, he took off his clothes and lay down upon the bed, thoroughly spent. He had never anticipated this ending to an evening intended to be a triumph. The opportunity to present his "proposition" to Anne had never presented itself, and now Max was faced with the reality that Anne might exit his life. His chest felt heavy, his whole being became anxious, and vague pains began to manifest throughout his body. *God*, he thought, *is the cancer becoming active again?*

Max decided to call Amy, whom he had asked to remain available for what he had hoped would be his triumphal call.

It had been his hope that he could tell his daughter that Anne was agreeable to his offer but, instead, he had to advise Amy that Anne was being interviewed for a movie offer and might be gone a year. Upon hearing this, Amy instantly offered to fly to New York and Max readily agreed. Max told Amy to take the first convenient flight the next day and to come to the Waldorf directly from the airport. Max told her that he would arrange for a room adjacent to his suite. Max then fell into bed, feeling utterly rejected by Anne and totally alone. For the first time since Anne had pulled him aboard her schooner, Max felt that life was no longer worth living. Although Anne had said to Max that she "would call in a few days," Max had a sense of foreboding that she might never call. Feeling totally defeated, Max at last fell asleep.

In due course, Amy arrived at the hotel and spent the remainder of that day resting from the effort to get across country as soon as possible. After a joyous reunion Amy went to her room after agreeing to meet with Max for breakfast in his suite the following morning.

Promptly at 9:00 A.M. on the following day, Amy knocked on her father's door and entered his suite where she took a seat at a table set up for breakfast for two.

Breakfast was ordered and delivered and soon father and daughter entered into excited, indeed almost confrontational, conversation. Three days had passed since Anne had sprung her surprise on Max, and Max had begun to regain the enthusiasm and optimism that had been his ever since that chance encounter at sea, which had saved his life.

Amy began, "Dad, you look wonderful. You look younger and stronger than you have in years. What is this woman doing to you? But first, Dad, tell me about the Amazon." Amy had not heard the details and wanted to know all about the Waoranis. Feeling justifiably proud that she had handled all his financial affairs during this bizarre episode in his life, she also wanted to let Max know that his estate was intact.

Max replied, "Amy, I will tell you the whole story in the next few days, but first I have to talk about my problem with Anne. Do you mind?"

Of course I mind, thought Amy, but ever loyal, she bravely replied. "Go ahead, Dad." Amy was jealous and she knew it. She feared that Anne might replace her in her father's affections.

Max said, "I must tell you first about my feelings toward Anne. She not only saved my life but has been my constant companion and inspiration these past months. It was this chance encounter at sea that made the Amazon adventure possible. Meeting Anne Arpels has changed my life and brought me hope for the future. I really believe I am in remission and that meeting her brought it about. Most importantly, we are in love. She has told me many times that she loves me, and I am madly in love with her. I had planned to ask her to live with me until I die and had planned to make her a generous offer until she told me about the movie deal. If she decides to make this movie in Italy, I won't see her for a year and anything might happen."

It was Amy's turn. "What offer did you make her, Dad?" Amy was insane with curiosity.

"Well," replied Max, "I have been thinking about this for months and spent an entire day in New York going over it. I was about to tell her a couple of evenings ago that I would leave her three-quarters of my estate if she would be my constant companion until I die. I also was going to say that it would be a personal arrangement of honor and that there would be no marriage. She was to be free to leave at any time and could do anything she wanted to do as long as she stayed with me. Of course, I would pay for everything and would give her anything she needed. The rest of my estate would go to you. An appropriate written agreement would be prepared to protect each party.''

Amy replied, ''Dad, what do you really know about this woman?'' Amy's face grew stern, and her voice took on a combative tinge as she sprang to the attack. ''You met her under impossible conditions; you know nothing about her family or her past life. What about her character? After all, she knows by now that you have a lot of money. You know, Dad, she could be nothing but a golddigger!''

Max looked fondly at his daughter. ''Please calm down, Amy,'' Max said. ''I know that she is a good person, intelligent, and that she comes from a fine family. She would never do anything to hurt me. It is just that, at this moment in her life, she has become excited about the possibility of becoming a movie star. She is a beautiful, twenty-two-year-old girl who apparently will be getting a glamorous offer to do something she has always wanted to do. Wait until you meet her.''

At that moment the phone rang. It was Anne. ''Good morning, Max. How are you?'' Anne sounded surprisingly cheerful. Max felt that the spat was over and that Anne was herself again.

''What have you been doing the past few days?'' he asked.

''Max, I have been in constant meetings all over town,'' she continued. ''I have been in meetings with producers, directors, reputed financial backers, script writers, and several Arab men who are introduced as 'potential financial investors' in the movie. I have even spent some time with a voice coach and some make-up specialists.''

''How did it go?'' asked Max, hoping for the worst.

''You won't believe what happened,'' said Anne.

''Just try me,'' responded Max.

''Okay,'' said Anne. ''But first I wanted to tell you that I love Chinese food!''

"You are trying to tease me, Anne," replied Max. "For God's sake, tell me what happened."

Anne continued, "Middy just called a few moments ago and told me that Stromboli could not get his financial backing. It seems that there is a problem about his financial statement. The deal if off. Can I come over?"

"Get your ass over here, Anne," Max replied. "I hope this isn't your idea of a practical joke. These past few days have been pure hell for me. By the way, Amy is here. She flew in from California a couple of days ago."

Max hurriedly had the suite cleaned and a fresh table prepared. He ordered fresh coffee brought up and sipped it while awaiting the arrival of Anne. Max looked at Amy. Her face had taken on a somber look. Max anticipated that a storm lurked ahead. Soon the doorbell rang and Max opened the door. Anne stood there, looking absolutely radiant in a smashing black pin-stripe business suit. She entered the room and they kissed passionately. Max began to cry and said, "Anne, how could you leave me?"

"Max," Anne replied, "it was a moment of madness. I'm yours; I will go any place you want." They kissed again and Max put his hands on her bottom. She playfully turned around, arched her buns seductively toward Max's face, and then sat down. Max was in heaven.

Amy could stand it no longer and shouted, "See, Dad. What did I tell you? She practically stuck her ass in your face!" It was only at the outburst that Max realized that he had not yet introduced Amy to Anne.

"Anne," he said, "I want to introduce you to my daughter, Amy. Amy, this is the woman who saved my life."

Amy was stunned. Never in her wildest imagination had she envisioned that such a beautiful creature could be the woman who had taken her father on this great adventure. She was obviously overmatched and, forcing a thin smile, she managed to say hello. Desperately trying to break the ice, Max said, "Look over the menu, Anne, and have some coffee." Anne soon told Max what she wanted and Max had her breakfast brought up. Amy sipped her coffee in stony silence. Anne sought reassurance by looking into Max's eyes. Inwardly, Max gloated over the manifest tug-of-war unfolding before his eyes. *It doesn't get any better than this,* he thought.

Just as Anne was about to begin breakfast, the phone rang. Max picked it up. Detective Michael Claiborne of the New York Police Department was on the line. "May I speak with Miss Anne Arpels?" he asked.

Max turned to Anne and said, "It is for you. It is the police department." A long conversation ensued during which Anne's face darkened as each moment went by. At length, she hung up the phone and returned to the breakfast table.

"What was that all about?" asked Max.

"Oh, Max, I feel so terrible!" replied Anne, who began to cry.

"Calm down, Anne, and tell me what Claiborne wanted."

At last, Anne was able to compose herself and began to speak. "The detective told me that he is on the Criminal Fraud Squad of the New York Police Department. He said that the department has been investigating a bogus Italian movie producer who has been in town for several weeks. It seems that his scheme is to contact all the beautiful girls in the modeling agencies in New York, offering parts in movies to be made in Italy. He arranges to fly these women to Florence, put them up in the finest hotels in the city, and then tell them that the movie has been postponed for financial difficulties. He then introduces these stranded models to Arab sheiks who offer the women enormous sums of money for sex. Of course, Stromboli is paid a handsome portion of the money for making these beautiful women both available and compromised. Several of the models are still missing. Claiborne has been ordered to contact all the modeling agencies in New York. Middy told him about me yesterday, so Claiborne called here to warm me. Max, I'm so ashamed."

Max pondered the situation for a few moments and said, "There is one thing I must know, Anne. Did Stromboli make a pass at you?"

"Please, Max, do we have to talk about it?"

"I want to know, one way or another," replied Max.

"Yes, he did," Anne said, practically shouting the words.

"I want to know exactly what happened," Max replied.

"On the day before I learned that Stromboli's financing was in trouble," Anne continued, "we had spent an entire day conducting interviews and meeting with several of his so-called financial backers. When the day ended, Stromboli took me to dinner at L'Etoile where we had one of the most glorious meals I have ever had. When the dinner ended, I expected him to take me back to my girlfriend's apartment, but he insisted upon going to his hotel for a nightcap. He said he wanted to read a particular portion of the movie script he was going to produce to me to see if I liked the story line.

"I agreed and we went to his apartment. We had a couple of brandies and, suddenly, Stromboli began to kiss me passionately and to fondle my body. He is a big, powerful man, and I knew that I was in trouble. Knowing I couldn't force my way out of the situation, I decided to trick him. 'Luca,' I said, 'if you want to get me in the mood, you have to clean up. Go take a shower and when you return, I will be ready."

Continuing, Anne said, "Stromboli rushed off to his bathroom and soon I could hear the shower running. Then he began to sing the opening bars of 'Torna A Sorrento,' and I knew my chance had come. I ran out of his apartment, slamming his front door as hard as I could, ran down two flights of stairs, and then took the elevator to the main floor. I yelled to the doorman to get me a cab and went immediately to my friend's apartment. This morning I received a call from Middy telling me the movie deal was postponed. You know the rest."

With tears in his eyes, Max grabbed Anne and kissed her. "Forget it, it's over," he said. "You are safe and we are together. That's all that matters. I will tell you our future plans later. Let's get ready to travel. We're off to Shambhala."

"Great," replied Anne. Looking toward Amy, Anne continued, "I'm all for it. But remember that old warning about three on a match."

Amy interjected, "Don't worry, Anne. Neither Dad nor I smoke."